KIDNAPPED IN DARK WATERS

CARLA CASSIDY

INTRIGUE

Recycling programs for this product may not exist in your area.

ISBN-13: 978-1-335-69060-9

Kidnapped in Dark Waters

For questions and comments about the quality of this book, please contact us at CustomerService@Harlequin.com.

Harlequin Enterprises ULC
22 Adelaide St. West, 41st Floor
Toronto, Ontario M5H 4E3, Canada
www.Harlequin.com

HarperCollins Publishers
Macken House, 39/40 Mayor Street Upper,
Dublin 1, D01 C9W8, Ireland
www.HarperCollins.com

Printed in Lithuania

"So, you won't help me," she said and then offered him a small smile.

"But I wouldn't be breaking any laws, so you also can't stop me, either." With that, she turned and headed toward the parking area.

"Dominique...wait," he called after her. But she didn't stop. She quickly disappeared into the twilight shadows of the night. Luke closed his door and returned to the recliner, where his thoughts filled with what had just happened.

He'd always found Dominique to be incredibly beautiful. He just hadn't known she would come up with the idea to tail a potential vicious murderer in the darkness of the night.

He didn't know Dominique well. Had this idea of hers only been an attempt to motivate him and the team to work harder on the murder case? Or did she really intend to follow through on her dangerous scheme?

Carla Cassidy is an award-winning, *New York Times* bestselling author who has written over 170 books, including 150 for Harlequin. She has won the Centennial Award from Romance Writers of America. Most recently she won the 2019 Write Touch Readers' Award for her Harlequin Intrigue title *Desperate Strangers*. Carla believes the only thing better than curling up with a good book is sitting down at the computer with a good story to write.

Books by Carla Cassidy

Harlequin Intrigue

A Bayou Investigation

Murder in Dark Waters
Kidnapped in Dark Waters

Marsh Mysteries

Stalked Through the Mist
Swamp Shadows
Hunted in the Reeds

Harlequin Romantic Suspense

The Scarecrow Murders

Killer in the Heartland
Guarding a Forbidden Love
The Cowboy Next Door
Stalker in the Storm

Visit the Author Profile page at Harlequin.com.

CAST OF CHARACTERS

Dominique Santori—Her mother was murdered and now she finds herself in the crosshairs of danger. Who can she trust?

Luke Madison—The handsome detective wants nothing more than to keep the beautiful Dominique alive. In doing so, will he also win her heart?

Austin Colbert—Is the librarian doing more than reading books? Is it possible he's reading books about kidnapping a woman?

Oliver LeBoeuf—Is the ex-boyfriend through with Dominique or does he have a sick obsession with her?

Jacob Benoit—Does the fisherman want to catch more than fish?

Burt Stanfield—He's one of Dominique's favorite diners at the café where she works. Does he want more than a meal from the beautiful waitress?

Chapter One

Mystique's Magic. The large purple lettering danced across a seafoam-green background on the sign above the front door of the store. A white banner hung just below it, with big red lettering announcing the grand opening.

Dominique Santori stood in a line of women waiting to get into the interior of the new, small store. The store was her older sister Angelique's lifelong dream, and a deep sense of pride filled Dominique at her sister's accomplishment. However, the pride and happiness she felt for her sister was tempered with a healthy dose of sadness and grief.

The store had been named after their mother, Mystique Santori. She'd been viciously murdered a little over two months ago and so far, there hadn't been any arrests for the crime.

She now smiled as she saw Monique, her younger sister, approaching where she stood. "Sorry I'm late," Monique said.

"When aren't you late," Dominique replied teasingly.

As usual, Monique looked sharp. She was clad in a long black-and-white-striped skirt with a ruffled white blouse. Her long, black hair was caught at the nape of her neck with a silver clasp and dainty silver earrings danced from her ears.

"Looks like she's got a good crowd," Monique said, obviously ignoring her sister's jab about always being late. "Have you heard anything from the women leaving the store? Any early reviews?"

"Not really, but I've heard snatches of conversations from the women standing in line behind me." Dominique released a deep sigh. "Some people apparently believe Angelique is setting herself up to become the next voodoo queen, since Mama is gone."

Before her murder, Mystique Santori was known as a voodoo queen both in the swamp and in the small town. People came to her under the cover of darkness to her shanty deep in the wetland that half surrounded the small Louisiana town of Dark Waters. It was whispered that she had dabbled in black magic, and most people in the town and swamp had been afraid of her.

"Well, that's just ridiculous," Monique scoffed. "Especially now that she's moved in with Daniel."

A little over a week ago, Angelique had left the swamp behind and moved in with the chief of police, Daniel LeCroix. The two had found love as Daniel had worked on solving their mother's murder. There might not be anyone behind bars yet, but Dominique knew Daniel was still hard at work trying to find out who took her mother's life.

"But you know how people love to talk," Dominique replied. "Still, it's an exciting day for Angelique and I hope she sells a ton of items today."

"I intend to buy something from her, but I'm just not sure what." The two women took several steps forward as the line moved closer to the door.

The two sisters small-talked and then they reached the

shop door and went inside. The interior smelled appealingly of a variety of florals and spices. On one side of the store were candles, bath salts and an assortment of other items for self-care.

On the other side was why Angelique had wanted to open the store in the first place. Shelves held a variety of poultices and tinctures and teas made from the healing plants and flowers from the swamp.

Angelique greeted both of them with hugs. "Thanks for coming in," she said, her face flushed with excitement. She was dressed in a pair of black slacks and a purple T-shirt with the store logo on the front. Her long black hair was in a high ponytail and tied up with a purple ribbon.

"We wouldn't have missed it," Monique said.

"How's it going?" Dominique asked.

"Better than I could have ever imagined. I've sold so much of the swamp-based items I'll need to head out to restock in the next day or two," Angelique replied.

"That's terrific," Dominique said. "We're here to shop, so we'll just look around while you take care of other customers."

Minutes later, Dominique paid for a candle and Monique bought some scented body lotion, and then together the two said their goodbyes to their sister and they left the store.

"Are you working today?" Monique asked once they were outside again.

"Yes, I'm on lunch duty today so I'm working from eleven to four," Dominique replied. "What about you?"

"I'm going in to work at five and I'll be there until close," Monique replied. "A new shipment is supposed to come in sometime this afternoon so at least I'll have something to do. I always love to unpack, inventory and then tag and hang new clothes."

"And you love to spend half your paycheck on the clothes you unpack," Dominique teased.

Monique laughed. "You aren't wrong."

"Then I guess I'll see you sometime tomorrow," Dominique said, eager to get into her car and out of the early August heat.

"Okay, sis. See you later," Monique replied.

Minutes later Dominique was in her car and headed home. She had a little less than an hour to get ready for her shift at the Dark Waters Café.

It wasn't long before she pulled up in front of the swamp's main entrance. She parked in the area where most of the people who lived in the swamp parked their cars and then she got out and headed into the thick tangle of greenery.

She half ran along the narrow path that would take her to the shanty where she'd grown up. Until a week ago, Angelique had lived there, but when Angelique had moved out, Dominique had moved in. The shanty was far bigger than the one where Dominique had been living and it filled her with the comfort of feeling as if she was home.

The shanty was one of the largest in the swamp, with three bedrooms, a bathroom, a living room and kitchen area. It was high on stilts above the water that half surrounded it. Tupelos and bald cypress trees rose up majestically around it.

Her mother had slept in one of the bedrooms, with all three girls in another. The third bedroom was where the 'voodoo queen' met her clients.

Once there, Dominique went into her bedroom and quickly changed out of the red blouse she'd had on and into the pink T-shirt that had Dark Waters Café printed across the front. Thank goodness she could wear her jeans to work.

Her bedroom was done up in the colors of a sunset. Her spread was in shades of deep pinks and oranges and matching curtains hung at the single window in the room. She loved this room, which had once been the bedroom she'd shared with her sisters. She'd always felt safe in here.

She pulled her long, dark hair into a high ponytail, sprayed on a spritz of her favorite perfume and then she was ready to go once again.

However, before she left, she walked to the door of her mother's bedroom…the room where her mother's body had been found by Angelique. Mystique had been in bed and her throat had been slashed.

Dominique opened the door of the room as a deep grief clutched at her heart. The bed was bare, but many of her mother's items were still there. At some point they all needed to be packed up or given away.

Her mother would never be there again to spray on her favorite perfume or read one of the books in the bookcase near the bed. She would never be there again to pull Dominique into a hug or share conversations about anything and everything. With a heavy sigh, Dominique left the room and headed for the front door.

It was time for her to get to work. Once again, she hurried down the narrow paths that would take her back to her car. Minutes later as she drove back into town, she shoved thoughts of her mother's murder away and instead focused on the workday to come.

Since it was Saturday, the café would be packed. But she didn't mind. She loved being a waitress and had a bunch of regular diners who always sat in her section.

She made good money in tips and couldn't imagine doing anything else.

She found a parking space in the lot at the back of the café and then went in through the back door. The people working in the kitchen all greeted her as she walked through to the small break room.

"Hey girl," Sunny Herbert, one of Dominique's good friends and coworker, greeted her. "Ready for another day in the trenches?"

"Always." Dominique placed her purse in one of the small lockers in the room and then pocketed the little key.

"I went into your sister's new store this morning. It's awesome. I bought a tea that's made from plants from the swamp and is supposed to help with cramps."

"Angelique is really into the plant and flower cures from the swamp," Dominique replied. "She's studied all about them. And now we'd better get out on the floor or Annie will have our heads."

Annie Fulbright was the owner of the café. She was in her mid-sixties and was a fair—but tough—boss. She had high standards and expected her staff to meet those standards.

The café was very attractive, with three of the walls painted by a local artist. The first wall was of pink bougainvillea flowers and the second was of majestic tupelo and bald cypress trees rising out of sunlit dark waters. Finally, the last wall was of the colorful storefronts that lined Main Street.

Within minutes, Dominique was busy taking orders and delivering food. She grinned as she greeted a man seated alone at one of the two-top tables. "Hey Burt, how are you feeling today?" Burt Stanfield was one of her regulars. The fortysomething man worked for the city in the maintenance department, and he was a widower. His wife had passed away two years before due to an advanced case of breast cancer.

"Fine as a fiddle, what about you?" he replied with a big smile.

"I'm doing just fine. So, what can I get for you today, Burt?" she asked.

"I'd like some coffee and the number three special. And even though it's a bit early, give me a slice of sweet potato pie. I've had a hankering for pie since the moment I woke up this morning."

"Then I'll make sure you get the biggest piece there is," Dominique replied. "You know I always take care of you, Burt."

"That's why I'm so crazy about you, doll," he replied with another one of his big smiles.

Dominique laughed. "I'll be right back with your coffee." She wished all her customers were as pleasant as Burt.

The next regular she waited on was Austin Colbert. Austin was in his thirties and was the town librarian. He always came in with a book and would read while he ate.

"Austin, how are you doing today?" she greeted him.

"Good now that I've seen your beautiful, smiling face," he replied.

"My goodness, Austin. You'll turn a girl's head with your shameless flirting," she replied with a laugh. "So, you want the usual?" The usual was a cheeseburger, fries and a diet cola.

"The usual is exactly what I want," he replied.

"I'll have that out to you in just a few minutes," she said and then left his table.

It was half an hour later when chief of police and future

brother-in-law Daniel and two of his men sat in a booth in her section. Dominique knew how hard the lawmen were working to solve her mother's murder, but so far it hadn't happened.

"Hi, Daniel," she greeted and then smiled at Luke Madison and Clay Caldwell. She had a bit of a crush on Luke, who she found ridiculously handsome, but she really didn't know him at all.

"Hey, Dominique," Daniel replied. "Your sister had a big morning."

Dominique smiled. "Yeah, I was at the store earlier. It appeared to be a huge success."

"It was, and Angelique is beyond thrilled," he replied. When he said her sister's name, his love for her was evident in his voice. Someday, Dominique would like to find a man who said her name with a wealth of love.

She took their orders and by the time they ate and left, the lunch rush hour was over and Annie sent her on a break. Instead of going into the break room where she usually took her breaks, she went out the front door, wanting to see her sister's store again.

From the café she could see Mystique's Magic in the distance. As she watched she saw two women walk out with shopping bags in their hands.

She was so proud of her older sister for working for and finally realizing her life's dream. Dominique's life's dream was far less spectacular. Eventually she wanted to be a wife and a mother. But she wasn't even dating anyone at the moment.

In fact, it had been almost a year since she'd had a relationship. At that time, she'd gone out on a couple of dates with Oliver LeBoeuf, who lived in the swamp and was a fisherman.

It hadn't taken her long to recognize that she liked Oliver a lot, but there were no real romantic feelings for him, so after about half a dozen dates, she'd broken things off with him. Since that time there hadn't been anyone.

She turned her gaze in the other direction, looking down to the popular dress shop, All That Jazz, where her younger sister Monique worked. And then she saw him. He was walking down the street toward the café.

Pierre Guidry. He had been her mother's on-again, off-again lover for years, and he was the man Dominique believed had murdered her mother. She also knew that according to Daniel, he was the number one suspect in the case but so far there wasn't any evidence to arrest him.

But Dominique had a plan to get the evidence required to get him under arrest. It would be dangerous, but she didn't care. She was determined to get her mother's murderer in jail and she would do whatever she could to make that happen, no matter how dangerous it was.

LUKE MADISON SAT in the small interview room that had been designated the murder room. Everything inside was dedicated to Mystique Santori's murder. His boss and good friend, Daniel LeCroix, was there along with Luke's other good friend and coworker, Clay Caldwell.

The three of them had worked almost exclusively for a little over two months to find Mystique's killer and get him behind bars. Their frustration with the case hung heavy in the air.

"I still think Pierre Guidry is the killer," Clay said. "It's the only thing that makes any sense. He went there on the night of the murder to get back together with Mystique. When she refused, he lost his temper and a fight ensued that resulted in him slashing her throat."

"Knowing and proving are two different things," Daniel reminded them.

They had interviewed everyone they could find who'd had dealings with the "voodoo queen," and they'd come up with two suspects… Pierre and a man named Charles Lathrop. Charles had come to Mystique for a love spell and when the spell hadn't worked, he'd been very angry with Mystique. But had he been angry enough to slash Mystique's throat? Pierre was by far the more likely suspect.

"So, where do we go from here?" Luke asked.

Daniel frowned. "We have no place to go. The case has stalled and unless somebody comes forward with some new information or the guilty party confesses, we're at a total standstill."

"How's Angelique taking it?" Luke asked. It had to be tough to be romantically involved with one of Mystique's daughters as the case grew cold.

"She's okay. She's frustrated as we all are, but she knows we're doing everything possible to catch her mother's murderer," Daniel replied. "Of course, she has her new store to focus on, which has helped."

"From the traffic going in and out, it looks like her grand opening was a huge success," Clay said.

"It was." Daniel looked at his watch and then back at his two officers. "And now it's time for you two to get out of here," Daniel said as he stood.

Luke and Clay got up from the table as well. It was just after five and time to head home. The men all said their goodbyes and then Luke walked down the long hallway that would take him out the back door.

The early August sun was hot on his shoulders, and now that he was off duty, he was eager to get home. Home for Luke was a two-bedroom suite in the Cypress Apartments. He'd been lucky to get a place in the fifteen-unit building. He'd been there for almost two years.

Eventually, he wanted to find a wife, buy a house and build a family. But so far, he was stuck on the *find a wife* part. He wasn't even dating anyone at the moment. In fact, it had been a little over a year since he'd had a relationship.

The apartment complex was only minutes away from the police station. When he reached it, he parked in his assigned spot and then got out of the car and went to apartment 107.

He went inside and walked through the living room and into the kitchen. He dropped his keys on top of the counter and then stripped off his gun and holster and placed them next to the keys.

He then headed down the hallway to his room. The neatly made-up queen-size bed was covered in a navy-blue spread, and matching curtains hung in the window. There was a dark walnut dresser and two matching end tables with small silver lamps on each one.

It took him only minutes to undress and get into the shower. The warm water didn't even begin to wash away the frustrations of Mystique's murder case. More than anything, they all wanted the guilty party to be caught and placed behind bars.

Once he got out of the shower he dressed in a pair of jeans and a gray T-shirt and then he went back to the kitchen. He grabbed a chicken dinner from the freezer and popped it into the microwave.

As he waited for it to cook, he sank down at the table. Lately, the silence in the evenings really pressed in on him. It was in the evenings that he wished he was married and had somebody to talk to…somebody to share his day with. So far, at thirty-one years old he hadn't found that special woman.

The microwave dinged and he ate. After cleaning up the kitchen, he went into the living room and sank down in a recliner chair.

It was Saturday night and time for him to call and check in with his brothers. Jerry was twenty-six years old and Brandon was twenty-four. Growing up, their father hadn't been in the picture and their mother had been a raging alcoholic. Luke had wound up being both mother and father to his two younger siblings.

Jerry now lived and worked in a warehouse in Shreveport and Brandon lived in New Orleans and worked as a waiter in a high-end restaurant. Their mother had passed away four years ago from acute alcoholism.

Luke made the calls, pleased that both of his brothers were doing well and sounded happy. Once that was done, he turned on his television. He tuned it to a crime drama and figured he'd watch a couple of episodes before going to bed.

He'd only been watching for a few minutes when a knock fell on his door. He frowned, wondering who it could be. Daniel used to drop by occasionally for a beer, but now the chief spent all his evenings with Angelique, the woman he loved—and Luke certainly didn't blame him.

He got up from his chair and went to the front door. When he opened it, he was surprised to see Dominique Santori. As always, she looked positively stunning. She was clad in a pair of jeans that hugged her long legs and a fitted pink blouse that enhanced her dark eyes and hair and showcased her slender waist and full breasts.

"Uh... Miss Santori, what can I do for you?" he asked curiously.

"Hi, Officer Madison. Could I come in and talk to you for a few minutes?" she asked.

"Of course, come on in." He held the door open wider to allow her inside and as she swept past him, he caught a whiff of her perfume. She smelled slightly mysterious and spicy, a scent he found very attractive. "Please have a seat." He gestured toward the sofa.

Once she was seated, he sat back down in his recliner facing her. She must have questions about the investigation, he thought. Before now, Angelique had always been the point person they all spoke to about the case. Maybe with Angelique busy with her new store, the sisters had decided Dominique would be the point person. Still, if that was the case, he wasn't sure why she'd ask him questions instead of going to Daniel.

"Uh...would you like something to drink? Maybe a soda or some iced tea?" he offered. Her black hair was loose and fell over her shoulders and down her back. The silky-looking strands only added to her attractiveness.

"No thanks, I'm fine," she said.

"What can I do for you, Miss Santori?"

"Please, make it Dominique." She smiled at him and the power of her beautiful smile formed an unexpected ball of warmth in the pit of Luke's stomach.

"Okay, Dominique, what can I do for you?" he asked, definitely intrigued by the unexpected visit.

"It isn't what you can do for me, but rather what I can do for you," she replied, intriguing him even more. She leaned forward, her chocolate-colored eyes flashing brightly.

"I think everyone is in agreement that Pierre Guidry

killed my mother, and there just isn't enough evidence to arrest him," she continued. "We also believe that whoever killed my mother stole the notebook she kept of her clients."

"Yeah, but we checked out Pierre's shanty and we didn't find the notebook there," Luke replied.

"Pierre is no dummy," she scoffed. "He wouldn't keep the book in his shanty where a police search would easily find it. He's smarter than that."

"Then where would he keep it?"

She sat back on the sofa. "He'd bury it. He once told me he buried all his important things all around the swamp. I believe he has my mother's book and he's buried it someplace. I also believe if I tail him, he'll eventually lead me to it."

"Whoa." Luke stopped her in alarm. "What do you mean by tailing him?"

"I'll secretly follow him when he's out of his shanty at night," she replied.

"Are you totally out of your mind?" Luke stared at her, appalled by what she apparently intended to do. "Pierre isn't some cream puff. He's a tough, strong gator-hunter and if what we believe is true, he's also a stone-cold killer."

Her cheeks flushed with color. "I know what he's capable of. I grew up with him in and out of our shanty. That's why I said I'd secretly follow him. I can move through the swamp like a ghost when I want to."

"Miss Santori—Dominique—I know how frustrated you must be with how long it's taking us to get your mother's killer behind bars, but the last thing you need to do is try to take the law into your own hands," he said.

The woman must be completely out of her mind to

even think about doing something like this. "You could be hurt or even killed," he added.

"That's why I'm here. I thought maybe you could act as my backup."

He stared at her in disbelief. "Why me? Why didn't you take this idea to Daniel?" Luke asked.

She flipped a strand of hair over her shoulder and frowned. Even with a scowl on her features, she was still quite lovely.

"I didn't go to Daniel because he would tell Angelique about my plan and I don't want to have a big fight with my sister." She leaned forward once again. "So, are you going to help me?"

"No, and I don't want you following through on this crazy plan," he replied. "Seriously, Dominique, if Pierre is guilty, then we'll eventually get him without you doing something so risky. Go home and leave the investigation to us."

"Are you sure you aren't going to help me?"

"Positive," he replied firmly.

"Then I guess I'm done here." She stood, her features radiating her unhappiness at his words. He got up from his chair and together they walked to his front door.

When they reached it, he opened it and then turned to her. "Good night, Dominique."

She nodded and swept past him and then turned back to gaze at him once again. "So, you won't help me," she said, and then offered him a small smile. "But I wouldn't be breaking any laws, so you also can't stop me, either." With that, she turned and headed toward the parking area.

"Dominque…wait," he called after her. But she didn't stop. She quickly disappeared into the twilight shadows of the night. Luke closed his door and returned to the recliner where his thoughts filled with what had just happened.

He'd always found Dominique to be incredibly beautiful with her long black hair and big brown eyes. He just hadn't known she was reckless, for that was the only explanation as to why she would possibly think tailing a potential vicious murderer in the darkness of the night was a good idea. Hell, Pierre could kill her and bury her body someplace in the swamp and nobody would ever be able to find her.

He leaned his head back and tried to relax, but relaxation was the last thing that was happening. He didn't know Dominique well. Had this idea of hers only been an attempt to motivate him and the team to work harder on the murder case? Or did she really intend to follow through on her harebrained scheme?

Chapter Two

There was no question that Dominique was disappointed that Luke wasn't going to help her, but she certainly didn't intend to let that stop her. Both of her sisters had always teased her about being impulsive, but this idea had been brewing in her head for the last two weeks or so. It was not an impulse…it was a plan.

She knew Pierre had a bad temper. She had grown up hearing the many fights Mother and Pierre would have. However, the arguments had never turned physical, at least not that she knew of. The two of them would fight and then make up, a pattern that had gone on for years.

When she and Pierre were off, then her mother would take another lover or two. However, she always wound up getting back together with Pierre.

But at the time of her murder, her mother had decided she was finished with Pierre for good, and Dominique believed that's what had driven him to kill her. But Dominique had no doubt that Pierre had loved her mother deeply.

She believed he'd taken her mother's client book in order to have a piece of her after death. And Dominique believed he would occasionally dig up the book and hold it tight against his chest as he mourned for the woman he had loved…the woman he had killed.

All she had to do was be there when it happened. Then she could tell Daniel about the book being in Pierre's possession and that would be enough to get him behind bars. It was a good plan.

When she got home from Luke's, she started her generator and then plugged in her phone to charge. She also got out a two-burner electric stovetop and for dinner she fried up a couple of pieces of fish and made a salad.

As she sat down to eat, an electric energy surged up inside her. It was very possible that tonight she could solve the crime and see Pierre arrested. That's all she wanted. Justice would be served and her mother would finally be able to rest in peace. And Dominique and her sisters would finally be at peace, as well.

By the time she finished dinner, she was wired for the night's events to come, but it was still a bit too early for her to get into place.

From years of knowing Pierre, she knew he did his gator-hunting and fishing a couple of hours after darkness had fallen each night.

While she waited for it to be time to leave, she changed into a pair of black slacks and a black T-shirt so that hopefully she could blend into the night without being seen.

Once darkness had completely fallen, she grabbed the pink-handled knife she carried for self-protection, then turned off her cell phone and slid it into her back pocket. Finally, she lit several of the battery-operated lanterns around the living room and then went out and turned the generator off.

It was time to go. Her heart beat a rhythm of nervous anticipation as she left her shanty. Just as she'd told

Luke, she moved silently through the marsh. She'd grown up running these trails and knew just where to step and where to jump to avoid the pools of water that occasionally obstructed her way.

Spanish moss laid ghostly, delicate fingers on her as she ducked under it and small nocturnal animals scurried along the brush on either side of her.

She finally reached Pierre's shanty, where she crouched down behind some thick brush in front. Light flowed out from the single window and she saw movement inside, letting her know he was still there and hadn't already left for his nighttime activities.

Her heart still beat quickly. This had to work. It had been too long with no closure in her mother's case, no closure for the three daughters who had loved Mystique so much.

Angelique had told her and Monique that the investigation had stalled. Hopefully in the next few nights, Dominique would be able to unstall it.

The moon was full overhead. It would let her see Pierre more clearly, but she was also aware that the silvery light would make it easier for her to be seen as well.

Her heart banged against her rib cage as Pierre's door flew open and he stepped outside. He was clad in jeans and a white T-shirt, and carried with him a snagging rod…a harpoon-type tool that was popular with all the gator-hunters. He also had a fishing pole and a large tackle box.

He probably had a gun as well. Dominique had grown up around enough of the tough men who made their living by catching gators to know it was a matter of pride to get one of the big beasts without having to shoot it. However, most of them carried a gun in case one of those big beasts needed to be killed quickly in order to save the hunter's life.

Angelique had told her that during one of Pierre's interviews with Daniel, he had mentioned that he had a sweet honey hole full of fish and one particular large gator that he was eager to catch. She figured that's where he was headed now. And it sounded like that would be a good place to have hidden the book he took from her mother on the night she'd been murdered.

She rose slightly from her position and nearly screamed as a hand clamped down firmly on her shoulder. She whirled around and in the moonlight she saw Luke, his brilliant green eyes burning with an anger that nearly stole her breath away.

He removed his hand from her shoulder and then gestured with a curt nod of his head for her to follow him. She looked back to see that Pierre had disappeared into the darkness of the night and she had no idea in what direction he'd gone. Damn, there was nothing more she could do than follow Luke as they made their way back to her shanty.

What was he doing here, anyway? Had he changed his mind about working with her? Doubtful. His gaze hadn't exactly radiated with "good partner" energy.

As she followed behind him, she couldn't help but notice his broad shoulders and slim hips. She'd always found him handsome with his slightly shaggy black hair, piercing green eyes and chiseled facial features. But she wasn't looking for a date, she was looking for a cohort to help her catch her mother's killer.

They reached her shanty and neither of them spoke as she unlocked the door and then allowed him inside. She sank down on the sofa while he remained standing.

"I really didn't think you would follow through with it," he said, his eyes still blazing with anger. "I was sure you would come to your senses and realize just how dangerous this idea of yours was."

"Then why are you here?" she asked.

"Because I also worried that there was a chance you wouldn't come to your senses," he replied. Some of the fire in his eyes dissipated a bit. "Seriously, Dominique, this is far too risky for you to do." He blew out a deep breath and sank down in the recliner facing her.

"This is necessary to get the evidence you need to arrest him. I truly believe that if he has it, he'll lead me to the book and that will be all the proof you need to get him behind bars," she replied fervently.

"We'll get the evidence we need without you putting your life in danger," he replied.

"When?" she shot back. "It's been a little over two months and you and I both know the case has stalled. It's on its way to becoming a cold case. Somebody has to do something."

"Well, it can't be you…not this way." He raked a hand through his hair, his frustration with her obvious. He drew in a deep breath and then released it slowly. "Dominique, I don't want to see you get hurt…or worse."

"That's not going to happen. I'm smart, Luke. I'm smart and I'm fast, and I'm quiet. Pierre will never know I'm following him."

He gazed at her for a long moment. "Is there nothing I can say to make you not do this?"

"Probably not," she confessed. She truly believed this was the only way to get the evidence necessary for the case. She had sat on the sidelines and allowed law enforcement to do everything they could and now it was time for more drastic measures. She truly believed she had a good plan that would lead to Pierre's arrest.

"Would you at least promise me that you aren't going to head back out there the moment I leave here tonight?" he asked.

"That I can promise you," she replied. There was no point in her trying to go back out tonight. The swamp was vast and she wouldn't have a clue where to find Pierre now.

He stood and she got up as well. Together they walked to her front door. He opened it and then turned back to her. "Can I get your promise that you'll put this idea away and wait for law enforcement to take care of things?"

"That I won't promise you," she replied. Standing this close to him, she noticed his scent. It was woodsy with a note of cedarwood and it was very appealing. "I'm sorry, Luke, but I have to do what I have to do for my own sanity. As long as my mother's killer is free, I can never really heal."

He frowned. "I know how hard this time has been for you and your sisters, but it would be a real tragedy if something happened to you. I'm sure your sisters don't want to see you doing anything this dangerous."

"It doesn't matter what my sisters think. This is my decision and mine alone," she replied. "Now, I'll just say good-night to you."

He frowned once again, the gesture doing nothing to take away from his handsomeness. "I still wish I could change your mind."

"Well, you can't," she replied firmly. "And if you were really worried about me, then you'd be my backup."

"I am concerned about you, but that doesn't mean I intend to be your partner in this foolish scheme. So, I guess this is good night." With that, he walked out of the door and quickly disappeared into the darkness outside.

Dominique closed and locked the door behind him, her thoughts scattered and disjointed. For a moment when he had grabbed her shoulder and she'd seen him, she'd hoped he was there to help her in her quest.

Was her idea really that crazy? She grabbed hold of one of the lanterns and went into the small third bedroom. This room held a compact round table and two chairs. It was here her mother would meet the clients who would come to her at night, seeking a spell or something else to heal them or somebody they loved.

One wall was covered with a dark blue scarf with the sun and the moon on it. A dark purple scarf also covered the top of the table. A bookcase held bottles and poultices, pieces of swamp plants and flowers and a variety of other items Mystique had used in her spells.

There was no question that her mother sometimes liked to play up her role as the voodoo queen, but her real power was in her knowledge and understanding of people and what they needed to feel better.

Dominique sank down at the table where her mother used to sit and a new, deep grief filled her. At the time of her death, Mystique was in perfect health and should have lived another thirty or forty years. She should have been at her daughters' weddings and held her grandchildren. Dominique and her sisters had been robbed of their mother's presence…of her love and support.

Mystique had been a spontaneous, free-spirited kind of woman. She was not a traditional parent, but she'd still been a wonderful mother who had always told her daughters how much they were loved by her. The only way

Dominique knew to keep her mother alive in her heart was to live her life just like her mother had.

The grief suddenly transformed to a deep anger. She wasn't about to give up on her quest to see Pierre behind bars. She had promised Luke she wouldn't go back out tonight to trail the man she believed killed her mother.

However, tomorrow night she would be back out there again, shadowing the gator-hunter in the darkness of the night.

"We have a big problem," Luke said to Clay and Daniel the next morning. The three of them were once again seated in the murder room.

"What kind of a big problem?" Daniel asked.

"A Dominique Santori problem," Luke replied, and then proceeded to explain to the others about Dominique coming to his apartment the night before and the discussion she'd had with him.

"I told her it was a dangerous idea and that she should leave the investigation to us, but I knew she wasn't listening to me." He continued to explain about going out and finding her crouched down in the darkness in front of Pierre's shanty.

"Damn, something like that could get her killed," Daniel replied with a deep frown. "If you recall, initially Angelique tried to meddle in the investigation."

"Yeah, but all she was doing was questioning potential suspects and you got her to stop. I'm not sure if anything will stop Dominique," Luke replied with frustration. "I tried to reason with her, but she's adamant that her plan will get us the evidence we need to get Pierre behind bars."

"We aren't even a hundred percent sure that Pierre is the killer," Daniel replied.

"Dominique is certain," Luke replied. "And she's also certain at some point in time he's going to dig up the book that he presumably stole and that will be the proof we need to arrest him."

"Well, we need to figure out a way to stop her," Daniel said.

"Good luck with that," Luke replied drily. "I got her to promise she'd stay in last night after I left her place, but I'm afraid she'll be back out there again tonight."

Daniel reared back in his chair. "The first thing I'll do is have Angelique talk to her. Maybe big sister can get her to stop with this crazy idea of hers."

"And if that doesn't work?"

Daniel eyed him for a long moment. "Then maybe you should partner up with her and see if you can keep her out of trouble and alive."

Luke stared at his boss in stunned surprise. "You're kidding me, right?"

"I'm not kidding. I would never forgive myself if something bad happened to my soon-to-be sister-in-law. Legally, we can't stop her from doing what she's doing, so the next best thing we can hope for is with you by her side she won't come to any harm," Daniel said.

Luke's head reeled as he considered what his new assignment would entail. "It's going to be difficult for me to be up half the night with Dominique and then show up here in the mornings for my normal shifts."

"We can arrange your shifts differently," Daniel replied.

Luke frowned thoughtfully. "I've got two weeks of vacation time coming to me. Why don't I just take it now so I can devote whatever time necessary to keep up with Dominique's nighttime activities?"

"I don't expect you to take your vacation time to work," Daniel protested.

"I don't have anything else planned, so I'll just take it and do a little bodyguard duty." The worst thing about this was the knowledge that he would have no set schedule. Normally, he was a stickler for structure but most of that would have to go out the window for now.

"Hopefully, Angelique will be able to talk some sense into Dominique and none of this will be necessary," Daniel said.

"Let's hope so," Luke replied. If Angelique couldn't turn her sister around, then Luke would be spending his vacation time babysitting a headstrong woman…albeit a beautiful one.

"I'll speak with Angelique as soon as I get back to my office and we should know how the wind blows soon after that," Daniel said.

"What do you really think about all this?" Clay asked him the minute Daniel had left the room.

Luke released a deep sigh. "I'm not sure what to think. On the one hand, I just want to do my normal job with the normal hours, but on the other hand, I don't want to even think about Dominique being out there in the dark all alone spying on a potential killer."

"Sounds to me like the Santori sisters are definitely a headstrong trio of women," Clay observed.

"I don't know about Monique and Angelique, but I can definitely say that Dominique is willful. I tried and tried to talk some sense into her last night, but she was having nothing to do with it."

Luke couldn't help but think about how beautiful she had looked the night before, with her dark brown eyes flashing and her chin thrust upward in stubborn defiance.

"At least her idea isn't a bad one," Clay said. "If we can tie that missing book to Pierre then that would be enough evidence for us to make an arrest and get him prosecuted for the crime."

"It might not be such a bad idea, but she definitely shouldn't be the one out there in the dark with a potential killer," Luke said.

Daniel returned to the room and sank down. "Okay, so I spoke to Angelique, who was positively appalled by her sister's plan. She was going to call Dominique the minute we hung up."

It was twenty minutes later when Angelique called back to tell Daniel that she'd been unable to make any headway with her sister.

When Daniel hung up from that call, he looked at Luke once again. "I would suggest you take off now and get some sleep before your bodyguard duties begin."

It was definitely a duty Luke didn't particularly want, but he would do it to the best of his ability, knowing that a woman's life could be at risk.

He got up from the table. "Then how about I officially take my vacation time starting now?"

"You know you don't have to do that," Daniel protested.

"I know, but it will actually make things a little easier on me," Luke replied. This way he wouldn't have to worry about working sporadic hours during the day. Hopefully, he would still be able to keep a routine of sorts. After the chaos of his childhood, routines were very important to him.

Minutes later, Luke left the police station and headed back home. Once there, he sank down in his recliner with the intention of catching a nap, but sleep was the furthest thing from his mind.

Instead, it was Dominique who took up residence in his thoughts. The woman was not only beautiful, but she'd smelled amazing, too. Her scent was one of mysterious spices and hints of florals. He had found it extremely attractive. He'd always thought she was gorgeous but he'd never asked her out on a date. He'd instinctively known she wasn't the type of woman he would want as a wife, so what would be the point in dating her?

He must have nodded off, for he awakened just before four. He stripped off his uniform, took a shower and then changed into a pair of jeans and a navy-blue T-shirt.

At six he fixed himself a sandwich with a handful of chips for dinner, and by six-thirty he was ready to leave the house and head to Dominique's shanty. It was plenty early enough that he knew she wouldn't have left for her spying duties yet.

Maybe it was possible he'd be able to distract her with conversation long enough that it would be too late to shadow Pierre. That might work for one night, but it certainly wouldn't work every night.

Perhaps she'd tire of this. After all, surely an attractive woman like her had better things to do with her time in the evenings. He had no idea if she was dating anyone, but if she was, undoubtably that person wouldn't want her out there putting her life at risk.

It didn't take him long to get to the area where the people living in the swamp kept their cars. He parked and got out. The swamp entrance itself was like a giant maw of dark greenery and tangled brush. It did not look inviting, but rather appeared forbidding.

Luke headed in. He carried with him a flashlight, although at this time of the evening it was unnecessary. He wore his shoulder holster and gun but he hoped he wouldn't have to shoot anyone before the night was over.

He walked quickly on the narrow path, dodging low-hanging tree limbs and Spanish moss. The air grew slightly cooler as he went deeper in where the sun couldn't shine through the thick leaves overhead.

Finally, Dominique's shanty came into view. He went across the bridge and then knocked on the front door. She answered the door and gazed at him in obvious surprise.

"Luke…what are you doing here?" she asked.

He forced a smile to his lips. He suddenly had a very bad feeling about all this. "You asked for a partner, so here I am."

Chapter Three

Dominique stared at him in surprise. He was the very last person on earth she'd expected to see this evening. "Are you going to let me in?" he asked.

"Oh, of course." She opened her door wider and as he swept past her, she caught a whiff of his delicious scent. "Would you like anything to drink?" She gestured him toward the sofa.

"No thanks, I'm good."

He certainly looked good. His jeans fit his long legs perfectly and his navy-blue T-shirt stretched taut across his broad shoulders and chest. His black hair was shiny and his green eyes were bright and alert. The shoulder holster and gun he wore made him look hot and slightly dangerous.

"Am I interrupting your dinner time?" he asked.

"I don't really have a specific dinner time and no, you aren't interrupting anything." She sank down in the chair facing him, still surprised by his presence. "So, are you really here to help me?"

"That's the plan. Daniel thought it was a good idea that I make sure you don't get yourself killed and I agreed with him."

"By the way, thanks a lot for getting Daniel involved

in this," she said with a touch of irritation. "My sisters paid me a visit this afternoon and practically took my head off. They couldn't believe what I intended to do, and tried their best to talk me out of it."

"Were they successful?" he asked, an obvious hope in his tone.

"No. Nothing and nobody is going to deter me from doing what I believe will prove that Pierre killed my mother." A wild grief shot through her. "You don't understand what it's like to know somebody is guilty and yet see them walking around freely and continuing to enjoy their life while the person they killed is dead and gone forever."

"I'm sorry, Dominique. I'm really sorry we haven't been able to get the justice you need for your mother." His gaze was so soft, and she wanted to fall into the green depths. He definitely had beautiful eyes. And for just a brief moment she wanted to be held in his big, strong arms as she grieved for the mother she had loved…the woman she had lost to a heinous crime.

"But we will get that justice for your mother and for you, if you could just be patient a little longer."

"I've been patient long enough," she replied and swallowed hard against her grief. "I know how diligently you all have been working on this, but you have to admit the investigation is going nowhere now."

"We are at a standstill at the moment," he slowly admitted. "But have you considered the possibility that maybe Pierre isn't guilty?"

"Yeah, I considered it and then completely dismissed it," she replied. "Pierre being the killer is the only thing that makes sense, and I know that he's your number one suspect, too."

"What if you follow him for days and days and he never digs up the missing book?" He leaned forward, his gaze once again intent on her.

"Then the only thing I'll lose is time and time is something I've got plenty of." She was aware of her chin shooting up in a tenacious fashion.

His gaze appeared to attempt to pierce through to her very soul. "Have you always been so stubborn?"

A small laugh escaped her. "If you asked my sisters, they would probably tell you yes. But I'm not stubborn, I'm determined—and there's a difference." She pushed a strand of errant hair behind her ear.

"I would beg to differ," he said.

"What would you know? You don't know anything about me or my life," she replied.

"Then tell me about you," he said.

She looked toward the window where twilight was falling, then looked back at Luke. Was one of his goals to distract her enough with conversation that she would miss the time to go out to tail Pierre? Well, that certainly wasn't going to happen.

There was no question he could be a big distraction if she allowed him to be. She couldn't remember when she'd last spent any time with a man, especially one as handsome as Luke.

"Do you have a special somebody in your life?" he asked.

"No…what about you?" If he was going to be her backup, then it wouldn't hurt for her to know a little bit more about him. Or so she tried to tell herself this was her only reason for asking.

"No, there's nobody in my life at the moment," he replied.

For some crazy reason that pleased her. Surely it was

just because it meant he would be available every night without having to answer to anyone at home.

"I know you waitress at the café. Do you like your job?" he asked.

"I love it. I really enjoy people and working at the café gives me an opportunity to visit with a lot of the towns-people I wouldn't ordinarily get to know."

"How are you going to be able to be awake for half the night and still work at the café?"

"I'll manage," she replied. Thankfully, there were many days when she worked the mid-shift, allowing her to sleep in a little bit in the mornings. "What about you? Why did you go into law enforcement?"

"A large part of the reason was Daniel. We've been friends since he and his dad moved here when Daniel was about eight years old. When he got the job as chief of police, he urged me to join the force. At the time I was kind of drifting and I didn't know what I wanted to do, so I wound up becoming a cop and I love it. It was the best thing I could have done for myself. I love the structure of the job and knowing the rules that need to be followed."

He sat back and frowned. "Sorry, that was probably way more information than you needed or wanted to know."

"Please don't apologize," she replied. "You know I have two sisters. What about you? Do you have any sib-lings?"

"Yeah, I have two younger brothers. They've both moved away from Dark Waters, but we're still very close," he said. "We talk to each other on the phone at least once a week."

"That's nice. Even though there are times they drive me crazy, I don't know what I'd do without my sisters.

The three of us are very close." Once again, she looked toward the window, aware of time ticking by.

"You three are very close in age. Was there ever any sibling rivalry?" he asked.

She wondered if he was really curious or simply trying to pass the time. "Never," she answered. "We have always been best friends and there was never any sibling rivalry between us. What about you and your brothers?"

"No, but I'm quite a bit older than them. I pretty much raised them when we were all growing up," he replied.

"Why is that? Where were your parents?"

"Oh, it's a long story and not all that interesting," he replied, obviously not wanting to share. "I've learned a lot about your mother during our investigation. Where is your father?" he asked, obviously changing the subject.

"The real question would be who is my father and I don't know. My mother never wanted to discuss the subject with us. We don't even know if the same man fathered all three of us, not that it ever mattered to us."

It had never really bothered Dominique that she didn't have a father in her life. "My mother was such a huge presence we never missed having a father."

She might be enjoying her conversation with Luke, but she remained aware of two things. The first was that he wasn't here to socialize with her. He was here because Daniel had probably ordered him to be here. This was a job to him and nothing more.

The second thing she remained aware of was that she wanted nothing more than for him to keep her safe as she hunted down the man who killed her mother.

"Even though a lot of people were frightened of your mother, I have spoken to a lot who sang her praises," he said. "From what we've learned, she helped a lot of people with her spells and chants and the natural medicines she gave them," Luke continued.

Dominique smiled, her heart greatly warmed by his words. "That's all Mama ever wanted to do. Despite the fact that a lot of people believed she used black magic and could curse people, they came to her because they needed some kind of help they weren't getting from any-place else."

The warmth his words had evoked inside her faded away as the familiar emotion of grief and anger took over. She stood. "It's time to go."

Luke looked at her with obvious disappointment. "Oh, and we were having such a nice conversation. Why can't we just stay here and continue to get to know each other better?"

"Officer Madison, this isn't a date. It isn't a social visit at all," she said. "You can either sit here and talk to your-self or you can come with me. The chitchat was nice, but it doesn't change my plans."

He stood as well. "I know from experience that I can be quite boring when I talk to myself, so I guess I'm going with you…and make it Luke."

She gave him a curt nod as her heartbeat quickened with thoughts of following Pierre. They left her shanty and stepped out into the bright moonlight. She turned to face him. "I'm going to be moving fast, so try to keep up—and for God's sake, try to be as quiet as possible."

With that, she turned back around and then took off down the narrow path.

LUKE FOLLOWED HER, grateful for the moonlight that il-luminated the path they traveled. She hadn't lied—she moved quickly and with a confidence he certainly didn't feel. It was obvious she was quite comfortable traversing through the wooded junglelike landscape.

Tension kept his muscles taut as adrenaline rushed through his body. He kept his eyes on her black-clad body and tried to move as quietly as she was. Still, he couldn't help but notice that she looked very hot in the skintight jeans and black T-shirt.

It wasn't in his job description to enjoy her company, but he had enjoyed the conversation they'd been having before they'd left the shanty. She'd waited on him often at the café and he'd always found her pleasant, but tonight she had revealed a lot more of herself to him.

Of course, she was nothing like the woman he eventually wanted to find for himself. She was far too…too spontaneous for him. She was right—his being here with her wasn't a date or a social event at all. His sole job was to keep her alive during her nightly activities.

They finally reached the area in front of Pierre's shanty where she crouched down behind a large thicket of brush and he crouched just behind her. It had been a very long time since he'd been with a woman and being so close to her awakened parts in him that had been dormant for far too long.

Her body heat radiated toward him and he could smell the heady scent of her. A couple of strands of her silky hair moved with a small breeze and caressed the side of his face.

He tried to stay focused on the shanty they were watching instead of the woman so close to him. Lanterns were lit in Pierre's shanty and moving shadows indicated that the gator-hunter was inside.

If Luke was lucky, Pierre wouldn't leave tonight. It would be far easier to keep Dominique safe if she wasn't trailing the man who might hear them or see them and react in a dangerous fashion.

If what they believed about the man was true, then he had already killed a woman in a vicious way by slicing her throat. What lengths would he go to in order to save himself from prison?

Unfortunately, after about twenty minutes of waiting, the man left his shanty. He carried with him a long spear-like tool, a fishing pole and a large tackle box. He headed down a path to the right of his house and Dominique and Luke quietly followed.

They kept bushes and thickets and some distance between themselves and Pierre. Thankfully, he didn't seem to be worried about how much noise he was making as he walked and so Luke figured it was less likely that he would hear their quiet progress behind him.

The going grew more difficult as Pierre continued on and the swamp became thicker and more challenging to travel. Luke lost track of time. There was only Dominique and the swamp and the man they were tailing.

Finally, they came to a large pool of water where Pierre set his things down and uncovered from the nearby brush a large pirogue. He put the shallow boat into the water, grabbed his items and added them, then he jumped in and took off, using the long tool to help him move away from the shore.

"Where are you, you bastard? I intend to get you tonight," Pierre yelled into the night.

Within moments he was out of their sight.

"What do you want to do now?" Luke whispered, hoping this would be the end of their nightly activities.

She turned to look at him, her dark eyes shining brightly

in the moonlight. "To wait. Eventually, he'll come back to shore. If you want to go on and leave, I won't blame you."

"I'll stay," he replied.

So, they waited. Small animals rustled through the brush all around them. Mosquitoes and insects buzzed and whirred in the air and a bullfrog croaked his deep-throated song. Fish jumped in the nearby water, and occasionally from the distance they could hear Pierre curse.

Minutes ticked by. Occasionally, they would change positions to be more comfortable. An hour passed and then another one. Although Luke felt like this whole idea of hers was a wild-goose chase, he couldn't help but admire her resolve in seeing it through.

They didn't talk while they waited. Having any kind of conversation would be a risk. What he was finding the most difficult was remaining so close to her. There was no question he was physically attracted to her and it was an attraction he hadn't expected to be so strong.

It was about two hours later when Pierre finally came back to shore. He got his items out of the pirogue and then hid the boat in the brush once again. He had a stringer full of fish and he immediately headed back to his shanty.

They followed some distance behind him. He made no stops and when he reached his shanty he went directly inside. As Luke followed Dominique on to her home, he could feel the disappointment that radiated from her.

When they reached her shanty, she turned to gaze at him. "Okay, so tonight was a big bust," she said.

"I'm sorry we didn't get what we needed tonight," he replied. He wasn't without sympathy for her. And of course, if she was successful in this quest, they would all get what they wanted…an arrest for the murder.

"Do you want to come in? I'm going to fry up some

eggs and make some toast. You're welcome to come in and eat with me," she said.

"You're going to eat now?" he asked in surprise. "But it's the middle of the night."

"It doesn't matter what time it is. I'm hungry and so I'm going to eat."

"Thanks for the invitation, but I always eat my dinner at around six each evening," he replied. "So, I'll just see you at the same time tomorrow night?"

"That's up to you," she replied. Her big brown eyes threatened to pull him in as the moonlight caressed her delicate features. God, she was so beautiful and for just a moment he wanted to pull her into his arms and take her lush lips with his.

The impulse shocked him and instead, he took a quick step back from her. "I'll be here tomorrow so don't leave without me," he said.

She half smiled at him. "Then don't be late."

He returned the smile. "I'm a punctual kind of guy. Good night, Dominique."

"Good night, Luke." With that she went into her shanty and he turned to leave.

As he headed back toward the entrance where he'd left his car, his thoughts were filled with the woman he had just left. Maybe she was right. It wasn't so much that she was stubborn, but rather she was determined.

No other women he knew would sit in the swamp for two long hours waiting for a killer to dig something up. He felt the weight of the investigation on his shoulders. If only the police could come up with the evidence they needed, then she wouldn't have to be out in the swamp waiting for a killer to make a mistake.

By the time he got to his car he was exhausted. Thank

God he didn't have to show up early the next morning at the police station for his shift. He'd go in about noon to check in with Daniel and let him know about tonight's events.

He certainly wouldn't share with his boss or anyone else how physically attracted he was to Dominique. There was no reason for anyone else to know that. After all, nothing would ever come of it.

THE NEXT MORNING, Luke got up at eight and took a long, hot shower. He couldn't remember the last time he had slept this late. He dressed in a pair of jeans and a dark green polo shirt and then left his place and headed to the police station.

His plan was to check in with Daniel and then eat lunch at the café around noon. He had no idea if Dominique would be working or not, but he was vaguely surprised to find himself looking forward to seeing her again.

Daniel was in his office and after knocking on the door, Luke entered. "So, how did it go last night?" Daniel asked.

"It went." Luke sank down in the chair across from his boss and then shared the events of his time with Dominique. "I'll say this, she's unlike any woman I've ever met before. She's very strong-minded."

"I have a feeling all three of Mystique's daughters are strong-minded. I know Angelique is. I think they all had to be in order to grow up with their mother's reputation hanging over their heads," Daniel replied.

"Yeah, it had to have been tough for them," Luke replied. He certainly knew how it was to grow up with people gossiping about a parent. He'd known from a very young age the terrible reputation his mother had around town.

"I know this isn't a duty you wanted, but I appreciate you going full speed ahead with it. The last thing I want is another dead body and I really don't know what Pierre is capable of if he were to catch Dominique spying on him."

"I don't want to find out," Luke replied darkly. "Anyway, I just figured I'd check in and let you know how it went last night."

"All I can say is keep doing what you're doing," Daniel replied.

"That's what I intend to do. I'll spend however much time in the swamp I need to in order to keep the lovely Dominique Santori alive."

"'The lovely'?" Daniel raised a dark eyebrow.

The heat of a flush filled Luke's cheeks. "I think we can agree that all the Santori sisters are quite lovely."

Daniel grinned and shook his head. "Take note, my friend. First, you notice how beautiful they are and then before you know it, they have you wrapped up in love knots and you can't imagine being without them."

Luke laughed. "That's not about to happen with me. Dominique is nothing like the woman I intend to eventually marry. She's just a job to me and she'll never be anything more."

Chapter Four

Dominique sat at a booth next to a window in the café. It was her day off and Angelique was supposed to be meeting her for lunch. Dominique was grateful that she didn't have to work that day because she was tired after the very late activities of the night before.

Sunny appeared at the booth. "So, who are you meeting for lunch today? I hope it's a very hot man who is madly in love with you."

"Don't I wish," Dominique replied drily. "You know there's no man in my life right now."

"And I also know how much you'd like to change that," Sunny replied.

"Yeah, well I'd also like to change my brown eyes to blue, but I don't see that happening anytime soon," Dominque said, making her friend laugh. "I'm actually meeting Angelique for lunch, but she's apparently running late."

"While you wait for her, would you like me to bring you something to drink?"

"A diet cola would be great."

"I'll be right back with it." Sunny left the booth and Dominique looked at the clock on the wall. Angelique was fifteen minutes late, which was unusual because normally she was quite punctual.

She looked out the window where the early August sun was bright in the sky. But she knew from reading the weather on her cell phone that the sunny skies weren't supposed to last and rain would move in later. She hoped the weather didn't interfere with her plans for the night.

Sunny returned with her drink and at the same time Dominique's phone rang. It was her sister. "Dominique, I'm so sorry, but I'm not going to be able to make it for lunch," she said.

"Is everything okay?" Dominique asked.

"Everything is fine except the girl I hired to run the store today didn't show, so I can't leave. Again, I'm so sorry."

"You don't have to apologize, sis. We can meet for lunch on another day."

"Yes, but I really wanted to talk to you today," Angelique replied.

"If you want to talk to me about my nightly plans, then you might as well hold your breath. I'm doing what I'm doing and no matter how much you try to change my mind, that isn't going to happen."

Angelique's deep sigh was audible. "Okay, then we'll just plan lunch for another day."

The two sisters said their goodbyes and Dominique hung up and then motioned to Sunny. "Looks like I'll be eating alone today, so I'm ready to order."

"Your sister couldn't make it?" Sunny asked.

"No, she can't get away from her store. The girl who was supposed to come in didn't show."

"Ah, business owner dilemmas. So, what can I get for you?"

"I'll take a club sandwich with french fries," Dominique said.

"You got it," Sunny replied and then once again left the booth.

Once she was gone, Dominique looked around. As usual, the café was busy and most of the seats were filled.

She waved at Burt and Austin, who were seated alone at different tables. They were definitely her favorite regulars. They were not only kind and respectful to her but they tipped generously, too.

She also nodded with a friendly smile at Oliver LeBoeuf, the last man she'd dated, who sat with two other men she knew were fellow fishermen.

He returned her smile with one of his own. Thank goodness after she broke up with him, they had managed to maintain a fairly friendly relationship.

As she gazed toward the entrance of the café, Luke walked in. He looked around and, spying her, headed toward her table.

He looked ridiculously handsome in his jeans and a dark green polo shirt that she knew would match his green eyes. "Hi, Dominique," he said as he reached her.

"Hi back at you," she replied. Despite all the scents in the café, she could smell him. The woodsy cologne he wore was exceedingly attractive.

He gestured toward the empty space in front of her. "Are you expecting somebody?"

"I was, but I'm not anymore," she replied. Why did her heartbeat always quicken when he was around? She wasn't even sure she liked him yet.

"Mind if I join you?"

She was vaguely surprised by his request. He would

be at her shanty tonight. Why would he want to spend his lunch time with her?

"Knock yourself out," she replied.

He slid into the booth and offered her a smile. "How is your day going?"

"It's going," she replied. "It's my day off and so far, I've been as lazy as a gator on a sunlit log."

He laughed, the sound low and pleasant. "I've been a bit lazy myself today."

Sunny appeared at the booth. "Hi, Officer Madison. Are you staying here and eating?"

He shot a quick look at Dominique and then looked back at Sunny. "I'm staying here and eating," he replied with one of his gorgeous smiles.

"Then what can I get for you?" Sunny asked.

"I'll take a cheeseburger and fries and an iced tea," he replied.

"I'll be back with both your orders." She gave Dominique a pointed look. "And we'll talk later."

"Why on earth would you want to sit with me?" she asked once Sunny was gone. "Didn't you get enough of me last night?" This close she could see that his green eyes had tiny flecks of gold in them. Definitely attractive.

"Why wouldn't I want to sit with you? You're beautiful and smart and I enjoyed your company last night," he replied.

She stared at him and he laughed. "Stop, you're looking at me like I'm a species from another planet," he said.

"I'm trying to figure out what kind of a man enjoys crouching down in a swamp for two hours," she replied.

He laughed once again. "Okay, I'll admit, I kind of hated that part of the evening, but before that I enjoyed the conversation we had."

"What're your plans for the rest of the afternoon?"

"I don't really have any. I hate not having a schedule. I like routine and structure."

It was her turn to release a laugh. "Then you're dancing with the wrong partner. The only schedule I keep is my work schedule. Other than that, I have no structure. Don't you have to go in to do regular police work?"

"I took two weeks of vacation time, so no, I'm not working my regular job at the moment."

She stared at him once again. "You took your vacation time so you could sit in the swamp with me every night?"

"Daniel and I figured it would be easier that way," he replied.

"Now I feel really guilty. Surely you had better things to do on your vacation."

"Actually, I didn't have any plans at all for it, so please don't feel guilty about a decision I made," he replied.

At that moment Sunny returned with Luke's drink and their food. "What else do you do with your time when you aren't waitressing or hunkering down in the swamp?" Luke asked. His beautiful green eyes pulled her in.

"I like to read and spend time with my sisters. I enjoy visiting with people and sometimes I have little gatherings of friends at my place, although I haven't done that since the murder."

As always, her heart squeezed tight with grief as she thought of the mother she had lost. "When Sunny and I are off at the same time we like to shop together. What about you? What do you do in your time off?"

"I also like to read, and occasionally me and a couple other men get together and have a beer at Jake's Place." Jake's was a small bar on the north side of town.

"I've never been there," she replied. "My sisters and I

always enjoyed going to the Voodoo Lounge." The Voodoo Lounge was a large bar with a big dance floor where lots of single people gathered on Friday and Saturday nights.

"Jake's is your typical dive bar. The drinks are strong and the food is greasy, but it's a good place just to unwind and talk. If you want, I could take you there one night."

"That might be fun," she replied. What exactly were they doing? They were talking as if they were a couple and that couldn't be further from the truth.

As they began to eat, they small-talked about things going on in the town and the people they both knew. Dominique found herself enjoying his company. He was not only easy on the eyes, but he also had a good sense of humor. He was very easy to talk to and then there was the simmering burn of physical attraction she had for him.

She had to keep reminding herself that she was just a job to him. He was probably cozying up to her in hopes he could talk her out of her plans with Pierre.

Well, that certainly wasn't going to happen. Until the police had somebody under arrest for her mother's murder, she intended to continue to shadow the number one suspect in the case.

"What are you doing after lunch?" he asked when they were finished eating and waiting for Sunny to bring their tabs.

"Going home and I think a nap might be in my plans," she said. "What about you?"

"Same," he replied.

At that moment, Sunny appeared. Luke tried to pay for Dominique's lunch, but she wouldn't allow it. Minutes later they walked out of the café together.

"This was pleasant," she said.

"It was very pleasant," he replied, his eyes sparkling brightly. "Then I guess I'll see you tonight."

"Same place, same time," she replied. "I'll see you then."

They parted ways to go to their cars. As she drove home, her thoughts were filled with the very handsome man she had just shared lunch with. Luke Madison. She hadn't expected to like him as much as she did.

She was definitely in the market to find that special man who she would love and who would love her. She wanted a husband and she wanted babies, but she knew Luke was nothing like the man she eventually wanted to be with forever.

Just from the brief conversations they had shared, she knew Luke was far too uptight for her. He was wed to structure and routine and she definitely wasn't. She wanted a man who could roll with her and be spontaneous. She intended to remain free-spirited and spontaneous as her mother had been.

"You're overthinking it all," she murmured to herself as she parked at the swamp's entrance. It had just been an unplanned lunch together.

She reminded herself that she was a job to him and he was nothing more than a bodyguard to her. They weren't dating. There was really no relationship except an odd sort of budding friendship between them.

She hadn't lied about a nap. That was definitely her plan for the afternoon. After that she would be ready for the night ahead and maybe this would be the night Pierre would dig up her mother's book and the case would finally be over.

She got out of her car and headed in to her shanty. The walk seemed unusually long today. The late hours of the night before were definitely weighing on her, although she would never admit that to anyone.

Despite her exhaustion, the surrounding swamp comforted her with the fragrances and look of home. It smelled green with the underlying scents of various flowers in bloom. There was also the rather unpleasant smell of decay, which she had gotten used to a long time ago.

The white piece of paper on her front door was visible from the bottom of her bridge. What on earth? She approached her door and pulled the note off. It read YOU WILL BELONG TO ME.

The letters were written in bright red with the word *will* underlined several times. A shiver crawled up her spine. She quickly shot a look around. Who had left it for her? She didn't see anyone lurking around.

She stared down at the note once again. What did it mean? With a chill flooding through her veins, she opened her door and quickly went inside. She locked the door behind her and then sank down on the sofa with the note still in her hand.

You will belong to me.

Even though the words themselves weren't exactly violent, it felt like a prophecy of danger.

As Luke drove home, his head was filled with thoughts of Dominique. She had looked so attractive in a brown sundress that was the exact chocolate color of her eyes. Her hair had been pulled back at the nape of her neck, exposing gold hoops at her ears. A gold necklace with a small locket had looked lovely against her medium skin tone.

There was no question that he had a smoldering desire for her. He hadn't expected that he would like her as much as he did. She was very easy to talk to and he found many things about her so interesting. She was like no other woman he'd ever dated before.

He pulled himself up short at this thought. But of course, he wasn't dating Dominique, and he would never be interested in dating her. He liked structure and routine, and she had said she had none. He couldn't imagine what it would be like to live with her. All he knew for certain was she was definitely the wrong woman for him.

He got back home and decided to take a note from her book and catch a nap. If last night was any indicator, the night to come would be long and probably frustrating.

He went into the kitchen and set his keys next to his holster and gun and then went into the living room and got into his recliner chair.

It didn't take him long to drift off to sleep and into dreams of his childhood. The dreams were snippets, moving quickly from one vision to another. His mother passed out on the living room floor…his brothers crying with hunger when there wasn't any food in the house. Angry banging on the door with the landlord wanting rent.

He woke up two hours later, surprised by the dreams that had tortured his sleep. It had been years since he'd had those particular visions while sleeping. What had brought them all back to him now?

Once he was awake, he spent the next hour seated at the table while he cleaned his gun. It was a task he didn't mind and one he did regularly. It hadn't been that long ago that he'd had to shoot a man.

When a suspect in Mystique's murder case was caught with meth-making materials in his shanty, he had wound up shooting Daniel and then Luke had shot him. Thankfully, Daniel had only been grazed in the shoulder and

Luke had shot the suspect in the leg, making it an easy arrest and nobody had died.

Once the gun was clean, it was dinner time. He pulled a frozen Salisbury steak dinner out of the freezer and popped it into the microwave. Not exactly a delicacy, but he didn't feel like cooking anything else.

When he was finished eating, he put on a clean pair of black jeans and a black T-shirt. Surveillance clothes, he thought with wry humor, although there was nothing humorous about what Dominique was doing.

By that time, he was ready to leave for Dominique's. Even though he had spent his lunch time with her, he still looked forward to seeing her again.

While he'd been inside, the skies had become angry looking. He hadn't heard the latest weather report, but it looked as if it might rain at any moment. Which wasn't all bad.

He would assume if it was raining then the night's activities would be canceled, and he could definitely live with that. It would be one less night he had to worry about Dominique's safety.

It still wasn't raining when he got out of his car at the swamp's entrance, but the air smelled like fresh ozone, letting him know the rain was coming very soon. The dark clouds swallowed up any twilight that might have occurred.

He turned on his flashlight to traverse the narrow paths, eager to get there and get inside before the skies opened up. When he reached the shanty, he knocked on the door.

"Who is it?" her voice called out.

He frowned in surprise. Last night she'd opened the

door without checking who it might be. "Dominique, it's me… Luke."

He heard the sound of the lock and then the door opened and she gestured him inside. Once he was in, she immediately locked the door after him.

She looked gorgeous in a billowing pale blue sundress. Apparently, she hadn't changed yet into her night-stalking clothes. Unlike last night, there was no smile on her face as she gestured him toward the sofa.

"Is everything all right?" he asked with concern.

"I'm not sure. Would you like something to drink?"

"No, I'm fine. Sit here next to me and tell me why you aren't sure that everything is okay." He patted the seat next to him.

She walked over to the bookcase in the room and picked up a piece of paper, then sat next to him on the sofa. "This was taped to my door when I got back here from lunch." She handed him the piece of paper.

He read it and a bit of concern washed over him. He set it down on the coffee table and then gazed at her. "You don't have a clue who might have left it for you?"

"Not a clue," she replied. "And I didn't see anyone around, either. I don't know if I should be afraid or not."

"It could be a threat," he said slowly. "It's also possible it's just a note from a secret admirer who plans to win your heart."

A frown furrowed her brow. "Then I don't like secret admirers."

"If that's all it is, do you have any idea who it might be?"

"I have no idea," she replied. "I've never understood the whole secret admirer thing. If somebody is into me, then step up…be a man and talk to me in person." Her eyes held his gaze. "This reminds me of what my sister went through."

Less than a month ago, Angelique had gotten a frightening note on her door. Then she'd been attacked by a person wielding a knife. The first time she'd managed to escape with just some wounds on her arm.

However, she had been attacked once again with near deadly results. The attacker had been Angelique's exboyfriend's new girlfriend. It had been solely based on jealousy and the belief that Angelique needed to die so the new girlfriend wouldn't have her as competition.

Luke reached out his hand and took Dominique's in his. "This is nothing like what happened to your sister, so get that idea right out of your mind."

Her cold fingers twined with his, as if she was seeking his warmth and support. "Just tell me…should I be afraid?"

With her big, doe-like eyes staring into his and her hand so small in his own, he wanted to promise he'd keep her safe forever. Instead, he really considered the situation before replying.

"I don't think you need to be overly frightened exactly, but I do think you need to be extra aware of your surroundings when you're out and about. This might be nothing more than a love note of sorts."

"Well, I'm not loving it," she replied drily.

"Could you get me a baggie big enough to hold the note? I'll take it into the station and see if we can lift some fingerprints off it. Hopefully that will tell us who left it."

"Sure, I'll be right back." She got up from the sofa and disappeared into the kitchen area. She returned a moment later with the baggie in hand. He carefully slid the note inside it and then set it back down on the coffee table.

"Now, on to more pleasant things," she said when he was finished. "Tell me what you did this afternoon."

"Nothing too exciting. I took a nap and then I cleaned my gun," he replied.

She raised one of her perfectly arched dark eyebrows. "Are you expecting a gunfight sometime soon?"

He was pleased that she appeared a little less tense than she'd been when he'd first arrived. "God, I hope not," he replied. "There's nothing a police officer hates more than having to shoot his gun."

"That is comforting to know," she replied. "I'm sure you all wish every conflict could be resolved easily and without violence. Speaking of conflicts, has anything happened in the investigation into my mother's murder?"

"Unfortunately, nothing has changed. However, it looks like it might pour rain at any minute. If it's raining, do you still intend to watch Pierre?" he asked.

"No. He won't go out if it's raining and so I think you're probably going to be off duty for the night," she replied. "And don't look so darned pleased about it," she added.

He laughed. "I can't help it that I'm not upset that we aren't going out to sit in a swamp for three hours or so."

"You know you don't have to do this." Once again, her gaze held his intently. Her eyes were so beautiful with their rich color and long dark lashes.

"Oh, but I do have to do this," he replied.

"Why? Because Daniel is making you?"

"Dominique, my need to go with you on your potentially dangerous nightly travels has nothing to do with Daniel. It has everything to do with the fact that I like you and don't want to see any harm come to you."

She offered him a small smile. "I like you, too."

Warmth swept through him, a warmth that enhanced the smoldering physical desire he felt toward her. He shoved the desire away as best he could. "Since you have no plans to go out tonight, I assume you're ready to kick me out of here."

Once again, she smiled. It was an impish grin that he found enchanting. "I could put up with your company for a little while longer if you want to stay."

He grinned back at her. "Then I guess I could put up with your company for a while longer, too." To make his point, he leaned back on the sofa.

"Tell me more about your family," she said. "You mentioned before that you have two younger brothers, but you said nothing about your parents except to tell me it was a long and boring story. We have all the time in the world tonight for a long story. So, are your parents still alive?"

Did he really want to talk to her about this? Maybe if he did, she would understand him a little bit better. "Like you, I didn't know my father, and my mother passed away four years ago."

"Oh, Luke, I'm so sorry," she said, genuine sympathy shining in her eyes.

"Don't be, it was a long time ago." He decided at that moment to tell her the whole ugly truth about his childhood. "My mother was a raging alcoholic who should have never had kids. I never knew where I'd find her. She'd pass out in the front yard or in the living room or in Swamp's End where somebody would eventually bring her home and dump her on the sidewalk."

Swamp's End was the third bar in Dark Waters. It was a small hole-in-the-wall that catered to a rough crowd.

Luke spoke fast, the words bubbling out of him as he recalled his childhood trauma. "She'd often forget about us and there wouldn't be any food in the house, or she'd bring home some random man who usually didn't want to see or hear me and my brothers. I did my best to take care of them, stealing food for them to eat and trying to hide them from those random guys. I'd get them cleaned up and dressed each morning and would walk them to school."

He drew in a deep breath and then continued. "It was a childhood of utter chaos. We never knew what to expect from one day...one minute to the next. The saddest part of all was when I heard she'd passed away, I felt nothing except the tragedy of a life wasted."

It was her turn to reach out and take his hand in hers. "Oh Luke, I'm so sorry you had to live through all that," she said softly.

He smiled. "It's like the old saying goes, something that doesn't kill you, makes you stronger. I now know what I'll do for my children to make them always feel loved and safe."

"So, you want children?" She released her hold on his hand.

"Eventually I'd like to have a couple, but only if I have a loving wife by my side. What about you? Do you want children?"

"Absolutely, but only if I have a loving husband by my side," she replied. "Right now, I'm not even dating anyone, so finding the man of my dreams might take a minute."

"I'm not dating either, so right now I'm stuck on the get-a-wife part," he replied.

She looked at him curiously. "Why aren't you dating? You're smart and have a good job, and you aren't hard to look at. I would think women would be clamoring for a date with you."

"I could say the same about you. You're obviously bright and witty and you are *definitely* not hard to look at. I would think there would be a long line of men wanting to date you," he replied.

"I've had a few men ask me out in the past, but they aren't men I'm interested in so I haven't gone out with them," she said.

"And I haven't met any women lately who I'm interested in going out with," he said.

At that moment the sound of the rain began to patter on the windows and roof. "The rain is upon us," he said.

"I love the rain," she replied. "I love the sound of it against the windows and the feel of it on my face. In fact, there's one thing I really like to do." She reached out and grabbed his hand and then stood and pulled him up with her. "Come with me," she said, an eager anticipation lighting up her features and sparkling in her eyes.

He let her lead him, curious as to what she had in mind. She unlocked and opened the front door and he gasped as she pulled him out into the rain.

"Follow me." She released his hand and ran down the bridge. He hurried after her. At least it was a cool, not cold, fairly gentle rain, but immediately he was soaked.

She reached the small clearing at the foot of the bridge and then turned back to face him. She laughed with what sounded like sheer abandonment. "I love to dance in the rain," she said. "So, let's dance."

She twirled around, a beautiful blue-clad nymph. She placed both her hands on his chest and smiled up at him. Her eyes glowed with pleasure. "Come on, Luke. Dance with me."

He was already soaking wet and her winsome plea resonated deep inside him. He took hold of her hands and they danced. They twirled and two-stepped and laughed with the sheer exuberance of it all.

He wasn't sure how long they had been dancing when she wound up pressed tight against him. The combination of the rain and her scent half dizzied him and her lush lips beckoned him as she gazed up at him. Suddenly, he couldn't help himself. He took her lips with his.

Chapter Five

She hadn't expected the kiss, but she welcomed it. She raised her arms around his neck and leaned into him. She opened her mouth to allow him to deepen the kiss. Their tongues swirled together and even the cool rain couldn't staunch her desire for him.

His lips were soft, yet held a masterful demand that was intoxicating. She could have kissed him forever, but after several minutes lightning slashed the sky, followed by a loud clap of thunder.

He pulled his lips from hers and instead grabbed her hand. "Come on, that's our cue to get back inside," he said.

He continued to hold her hand as they ran up the bridge and back into the shanty. Only then did he drop her hand from his. "Towels," she said. "Stay there and I'll be right back."

She disappeared into the bathroom and returned carrying two large fluffy red towels. She handed him one and for a moment they dried off.

He ran the towel over his hair and clothes. "What do you want me to do with the towel?" he asked.

"I'll take it."

She took it from him and then went back into the bathroom. “I’m sorry I don’t have a dryer to take care of your wet clothes,” she said when she came back into the living room.

“It’s okay. I’ll just head on home and throw them in mine,” he replied.

“Thank you for dancing with me, Luke,” she said with a wide smile.

“I’ve never done anything like that before in my life,” he replied. “I’ve never even thought about doing anything like that before.”

“Tell me the truth—it was fun, wasn’t it?”

He laughed. “I’ll admit, it was fun and now I’ll just say good-night and I’ll see you tomorrow.” He walked over to the coffee table and picked up the baggie holding the note and then he disappeared out the front door.

It was only after he was gone that she thought about the fact that he hadn’t mentioned their kiss. Had it meant nothing to him? She didn’t even know what it meant to her. All she did know was it had been an awesome kiss.

She went into her bedroom and took off the wet dress and underwear and pulled on a navy-blue nightshirt. She walked back into the living room and sank down on the sofa, the kiss still very much on her mind.

She couldn’t know what he thought about it, but for her it had been absolutely magical. His lips had been so warm and inviting on hers and she couldn’t wait for an opportunity to kiss him again.

Her gaze dropped to the coffee table as she thought about the note that had been on her door. *You will belong to me.* Who had left it for her? And what exactly did it mean?

Was it really just an odd love note of sorts or something more ominous? How afraid should she really be?

She definitely intended to be more aware of her surroundings and not let anyone get too close to her.

Her thoughts jumped to those moments when Luke had shared the tragedy of his past. It had broken her heart for him as she'd heard about his mother. It had also shown her what kind of a man he was to take care of his younger brothers' needs above his own.

He was a special kind of man, but he wasn't her special man. She might have gotten him to dance in the rain with her, but she had a feeling he was too uptight…too regimented in his day-to-day life to be a good fit for her.

She double-checked that her doors were locked up and then got into bed. The rain still pitter-pattered on her window, the sound lulling her to sleep. She fell into dreams of dancing in the rain with Luke.

THE NEXT MORNING, the plan was to go to breakfast with her sisters. She was on the dinner shift and Monique was working later that afternoon at the dress shop. Hopefully, Angelique could get away from the store to meet with them. It had been a minute since the three of them had gotten together.

The first thing she did was drape all the wet things from the night before over her railing outside. There was no sign of rain today and the sun was nice and bright and would dry the towels and her sundress in no time.

She dressed in a pair of jeans and a red-and-blue blouse. She pulled her long hair back and tied it at the nape of her neck with a red ribbon. She applied a little makeup and then spritzed on her favorite scent.

At the last minute, she got the knife she carried at night and put it in her purse. Hopefully, she wouldn't have to stab anyone. However, as she thought of that note, she wanted to have something for her own protection in case somebody came at her sideways.

As she walked through the swamp, she kept her gaze shooting all around and listened to make sure nobody was sneaking up on her. She breathed a sigh of relief as she broke into the clearing where her car was parked.

Monique was already there. Clad in a pair of jeans and a turquoise blouse, she looked absolutely beautiful. "Hey, girl." Monique greeted her with a big smile.

"You look very pretty," Dominique said.

"Thanks, sis," Monique replied. "So do you."

The two of them got into Dominique's car. "Have you heard anything from Angelique this morning?" Dominique asked as she started the engine.

"I spoke to her about twenty minutes ago. She was at her store, and the new girl who started working for her was also there so she said she would meet us at the café," Monique said.

"Good. Last time she was supposed to meet me, she didn't show because of staffing issues." Instead, she had enjoyed her lunch with Luke. "I've missed the three of us getting together."

"Yeah, me too. But with all of us working different hours, it's hard to coordinate," Monique replied.

"Speaking of work, how are things going at the dress shop?"

"Really well. Debbie has stepped away and rarely comes in anymore. I think she's about to make me a full-time manager." Debbie Waltrip, a woman who was retirement age, owned the All That Jazz dress shop.

"That's exciting. Are you ready for all the responsibility that would come with that?"

"Definitely. It's nice that I love working there so much," Monique replied.

"Debbie is lucky to have you. I'm sure you're her top seller. You are so good with the customers."

Monique laughed. "If you're trying to make me feel good about myself this morning, it's working."

"Yeah, just don't get a big head," Dominique replied, making Monique laugh once again.

They chitchatted for a few more minutes until they reached the café. Dominique parked and it didn't take them long to be seated in a booth.

Sunny approached them. "Good morning, ladies," she said brightly. "What can I start you off with? Coffee? Juice?"

"We're waiting on Angelique, but in the meantime, I'd love a cup of coffee," Dominique said.

"Make that two," Monique added.

"I'll be right back with those." She left the booth and before she could deliver the coffee, Angelique arrived. She slid in next to Monique and greeted them. She was dressed in a pair of black slacks and one of the purple T-shirts with her store logo on the front.

"Glad you could make it," Dominique said.

"I finally have a nice, responsible young woman working for me," Angelique replied.

"That's good because you occasionally need to get away from the store and have breakfast with your sisters," Monique said.

Angelique grinned with good humor. Within minutes all three had coffee and had ordered their food. As they waited, they talked about the things going on in their lives.

Dominique hadn't decided yet if she was going to share

the note she'd received. The last thing she wanted to do was worry her sisters. They were already worried enough about her shadowing Pierre at night, although they were pleased that Luke was going with her when she went out to catch their mother's killer.

She looked around the café. Was the man who left the note for her sitting in here right now? She didn't see anyone paying any particular attention to her.

Sunny arrived with their food. Dominique had ordered pancakes this morning while Monique had ordered an omelet and Angelique the French toast. They were definitely different when it came to their favorite breakfast meals.

As they ate, they continued to catch up with each other. What they didn't discuss was their mother's murder or the investigation. There was nothing more to say about either subject as they all just hoped an arrest would be made very soon and the killer would finally face justice.

There were still days when Dominique's grief over the loss of her mother would rear up and threaten to consume her, but those days were coming less frequently now. Time truly was a healer.

"Girls, it's so nice to see you all three together." Nola Fontenot stopped by the side of their booth. "Your mother must be smiling down from Heaven knowing the three of you are all together," the plump, brown-haired woman said.

Nola had been Mystique's closest friend and was like a favorite aunt to the sisters. "How are you doing, Nola?" Dominique asked.

"Oh, you know, I still have days of grief. I miss your mother like crazy," she replied.

"We all do," Angelique said.

"I just wish Daniel would get that damned Pierre under

arrest, because I truly believe that man is responsible for her death." Nola grimaced. "I don't know what's taking him so long."

"Daniel is doing the very best he can to catch Mama's murderer." Angelique quickly jumped to her lover's defense. "Right now, he lacks enough evidence to arrest Pierre, but trust me, he and his men are working hard on the case."

"I just hate seeing that man walking around like he doesn't have a care in the world. I guess I'm just an impatient ninny," Nola said with a small laugh. "And now I'll just let you all finish your breakfast."

She left their booth and headed to the other side of the café, where two women awaited her at a four-top table. "She's as anxious as we are to get this case solved," Angelique said and then looked pointedly at Dominique. "That doesn't mean I want my sister out there watching Pierre in the dead of night."

"I'm perfectly safe in what I'm doing with Luke by my side," Dominique replied. "He's a very good bodyguard and last night I even got him to dance in the rain with me."

Both her sisters stared at her in obvious surprise. "You got Luke Madison to dance in the rain with you?" Angelique shook her head and released a small laugh. "From what I've heard, that man is so uptight he squeaks when he walks."

"You like him," Monique said.

"I do like him," Dominique replied.

"No, I mean you really like him." Monique held Dominique's gaze.

"I suppose you could do a whole lot worse than Luke," Angelique added.

Dominique laughed. "Luke is a likeable guy. He's my

partner and nothing more. He is too regimented for me, and I'm too spontaneous and free for him. If we were romantically together, we'd probably kill each other within twenty-four hours."

"You're probably right about that," Angelique said.

They all finished eating and paid, and within minutes Angelique was headed back to her shop and Dominique and Monique were back in the car and heading home.

"This was nice," Monique said. "I always like it when the three of us get together."

Dominique shot a quick look at her sister. Her younger sister was the softest of the three. She often kept her thoughts to herself. She was rather shy and quiet unless she was at work or on the dance floor at the Voodoo Lounge. Dominique might have danced in the rain last night with Luke, but Monique definitely came alive when she was dancing.

"When are you going to find some nice man to date?" Dominique asked.

Monique laughed. "Remember, I'm younger than you so I'm in no real hurry to find a nice man."

"You're only a little over a year younger than me," Dominique replied.

Monique grinned at her and then sobered. "Seriously, Dominique, I have my work and right now that's enough for me. I know you and Angelique worry about me, but really, I'm doing just fine. However, I'll be better once Mama's killer is behind bars and there's true closure to the case. Right now, it's just a festering wound."

"I think we'll all do better after that happens," Dominique agreed. They arrived at the swamp entrance, got out of the car and headed in.

When they reached Monique's shanty, they said their

goodbyes and hugged and then Dominique continued on her way. Just as she had when she'd left, she kept an eye out for anyone else who might be on the path with her.

As she walked, her thoughts went to the brief conversation they'd had about Luke. Immediately, the memory of the very hot kiss she'd shared with him warmed her from head to toe.

Surely, Luke's kiss had seemed unusually hot only because it had been a very long time since she'd kissed a man. Oliver LeBouef's kisses sure hadn't been as hot... as wonderful as Luke's had been.

Would he kiss her again tonight? A shiver of sweet anticipation shot through her. She entered her shanty and shut and locked the door behind her.

What in the hell was she doing? Why would she want a man who was definitely all wrong for her to kiss her again?

THAT KISS...THAT VERY hot kiss with Dominique had been on Luke's mind from the moment he had gotten home from her place last night and still teased and tormented him long after he'd awakened that morning.

She had tasted of sweet, hot desire and if that lightning bolt hadn't slashed the dark skies overhead, he had no idea where the kissing might have led.

Now that he'd tasted the sweet heat of her mouth, he was definitely tempted to kiss her again and again. But that couldn't happen.

Nothing good would come of kissing her, except it would feed his physical desire for her and he couldn't allow that to dictate where their relationship went. They had no real relationship except they were friendly with each other and he had the task of keeping her alive.

The other thing that had been on his mind was the note that had been left for her. Did it indicate she was in danger? His gut instinct told him no, that it probably was the work of a secret admirer. But could he trust his gut instinct?

Still, he intended to remind her that night when he saw her again that she needed to stay aware of her surroundings. There was no way to know what the note writer had in mind, so it was best to err on the side of caution.

At the moment, he was on his way into the police station to do a check-in with Daniel. It was just after lunch time and there was no hint of the rainstorm that had swept the area the night before.

If anyone would have told him that there would come a night when he would dance in the rain with Dominique Santori, he wouldn't have believed them. It was so far out of character for him and yet he had to admit it had been exhilarating and more fun than he could remember enjoying in a very long time. The truth was he had to admit there wasn't much fun in his life.

He pulled up behind the police station and parked in the lot, then entered through the back door. He didn't see any other officers as he walked down the long hallway toward Daniel's office.

Most of them would be out on patrol, except for Gus Smith. The older officer was near retirement age and also suffered from severe arthritis in his hips. He worked the day shift as the receptionist.

Luke went into the murder room and set the baggie-clad note on the table and then continued on down the hallway.

When he reached Daniel's office, he knocked on the

door. Daniel immediately called out for him to enter and Luke did just that. "Hey, boss," he greeted Daniel.

"Luke, how are you doing?"

Luke sat in the chair in front of Daniel's desk. "I'm doing all right. I just figured I'd do a quick check-in even though I don't have anything to report. Thankfully, the rain kept Dominique from trying to follow Pierre last night."

"Yeah, Angelique had breakfast with her sisters this morning, and Dominique shared with them about your night activities." Daniel raised a brow as a wry smile curved his lips. "Dancing in the rain, Luke? I didn't know you had it in you."

The warmth of a blush filled Luke's cheeks. He hadn't intended sharing that fact with anyone, especially Daniel. "Yeah, I didn't know I had it in me, either. It started to rain and she grabbed my hand and pulled me outside and before I knew it, we were dancing."

The smile on Daniel's face fell away. "A word of advice, Luke. Remember, she is just a job. I've known you for years, and I really don't think she's the type of woman you need in your life."

"I'm not looking at being a lifelong partner with her, and believe me, she really is just a job to me, although we are friendly with each other." At least, thank God, she apparently hadn't shared the fact they had kissed.

"There is one other thing that happened to her yesterday." Luke told Daniel about the note she had received. "It sounds to me like she's picked up a secret admirer, but I did tell her she needed to stay aware of her surroundings and who she allows to get close to her. I also brought the note in to see if we could lift any prints from it. I left it on the table in the murder room."

"I'll have Clay grab it," Daniel replied. Clay was their number one expert in fingerprint retrieval. "In the meantime, there isn't much we can do about the note, however, you were absolutely right to tell Dominique to watch her surroundings and hopefully the writer of the note is nothing more than a lovesick individual who means no harm."

"Let's hope," Luke replied. "Anyway, that's my report for the day. Anything new on Mystique's murder case?"

Daniel frowned. "Unfortunately, no. We still have no leads to follow at the moment."

"If I really see Pierre dig up the missing client book, do you want me to make an arrest right then and there?"

"No, I want you to call for backup and then we'll take him down," Daniel replied.

"Got it. And on that note, I'll just get out of here." Luke stood.

"Any plans for the afternoon?" Daniel asked.

"Yeah, a nap. I don't think it's going to rain again, so Dominique will want to follow Pierre again tonight."

"Then have a good nap. I imagine you'll need it," Daniel replied.

"Thanks, and I'll see you tomorrow." Luke left the office and walked back out of the building and into the summer heat. As he drove home, his thoughts were a jumble.

His physical desire for Dominique battled with his sense of duty. Then there was the note she received that might or might not portend some sort of coming conflict.

If it truly was from a secret admirer, when they made themselves known to her, would she be thrilled about the person's identity? Would it be from someone she was excited to date? That thought sparked a surprising touch of jealousy inside him…a jealousy that had no place in his thoughts or in his relationship with the beautiful woman.

By the time he was home, he was ready for a nap and it didn't take him long to fall asleep in his recliner. He slept with no dreams and awakened about two hours later, just in time to make dinner.

He had decided to cook tonight, and had a nice steak marinating in his refrigerator. That along with a baked potato was dinner.

After eating, he cleaned up the kitchen and then went to his bedroom to change into his night-stalking clothing. Once he was dressed, he left the house to head to the swamp. It was a bit earlier than usual. However, he'd rather wait for night to fall at her house with her company instead of sitting in the silence of his own place.

As he drove, a sweet anticipation filled him at the thought of spending more time with her. *She's just a job*, he reminded himself. But he'd never enjoyed a job as much as he was enjoying this one.

She fascinated him. She was so different from any other woman he'd ever known. He was interested in knowing everything about her. That didn't mean he was entertaining any real feelings for her except a deep curiosity.

He reached the swamp entrance and parked and then got out of his car and headed in. The sunlight was still fairly bright overhead but it wouldn't be long before twilight fell.

He walked briskly, more comfortable since he'd become more familiar with the path to her place. As always small animals scampered in the brush and insects buzzed and whirred in the air.

Maybe tonight would be the night she would give up this dangerous job she'd set for herself. What if Pierre hadn't buried the book? Luke still didn't understand why the man would have wanted Mystique's client book to begin with, but the facts indicated the book had been stolen on the night of the murder. And Luke did believe Pierre was their murderer.

He shoved all these thoughts out of his head as he reached her front door. He knocked. "Dominique, it's me."

He heard her unlock her front door and then she opened it and gestured him inside. As usual, even though she was once again clad in the tight black jeans and a black T-shirt, she looked stunning. Her hair was pulled back at the nape of her neck, emphasizing her high cheekbones and beautiful features.

"Hi," he said as he walked over to the sofa and sat.

"Hi yourself," she replied and sat next to him, bringing with her the wonderful scent that he now identified as hers alone.

"How was your day?" he asked.

"It was okay. I had breakfast with my sisters, which is always nice. After that I worked the lunch shift at the café and I got back here just after four. How was your day?"

"Fairly quiet. I spent the morning doing a little cleaning and then this afternoon I went into the police station and spoke with Daniel. I also dropped off the note you got for fingerprinting."

"Hopefully they'll find some. Still no movement on my mother's case?" she asked. Her beautiful eyes held his gaze and he wished he could tell her something, anything that would take away the haunting he saw in the depths there.

"Nothing," he finally replied. "But that doesn't mean something couldn't break loose at any time."

Her gaze turned skeptical. "And tomorrow gators will learn how to speak English."

"My scenario is much more realistic than yours," he replied with a small laugh.

She grinned at him, that impish smile that always charmed him. "Let's hope you're right."

"The day that gators speak English, I'll jump in the swamp and eat only insects."

She laughed. He loved the sound of her laughter. It was low-pitched and musical. For the next hour they small-talked. He learned several more things about her.

Her favorite music was old rock and roll, the same kind he liked. She loved shrimp while he preferred a good burger. She believed in UFO's, and he wasn't sure he believed in extraterrestrial beings.

All too quickly, she was ready to leave the cabin and head out to Pierre's shanty. "I wish you didn't believe this was necessary," he said as they walked out into the darkness of the night. She paused at the top of the bridge and turned to him.

"But I do think it's necessary," she replied softly. Her eyes glowed in the moonlight. "It's been over two months since Angelique found our mother dead…murdered in her bed. Over two months with no closure. Over two months with no justice. Luke, I have to do this, otherwise I'd go crazy just sitting and waiting around for something to happen."

"Then let's go," he said gently. She smiled at him gratefully and together they went across the bridge and into the tangled greenery of the swamp.

He followed her on the path to Pierre's place. When they reached it, they crouched down behind the bushes where they had hidden the last time.

Lantern light spilled out of Pierre's window and shadowy movement let him know the gator-hunter hadn't left yet. Like the last time, as they waited for Pierre to make a move, he couldn't help but be far too aware of Dominique's nearness.

His physical desire for her reared up and he had to consciously tamp it down. It had no place in their relationship. They were merely friends doing a job together, and that was all. He just had to keep her from harm, and that was the beginning and the ending of their relationship.

It wasn't long before Pierre left his shanty. He carried the same items he had before and he seemed to be in no hurry as he took off down a path.

Luke and Dominique followed him closely, keeping brush and trees between them. They hadn't gone far when Luke accidentally stepped on a dead tree limb that snapped loudly.

Pierre stopped in his tracks, his head swiveling slowly from right to left. *Damn.* Luke froze in place, as did Dominique as the gator-hunter seemed to look right at them.

Chapter Six

Dominque's breath caught in the back of her throat. The snapping limb had sounded like a gunshot in the relative quiet of the night. It had certainly drawn the unwanted attention of Pierre.

Her heartbeat thundered as Pierre stared in their direction. Could he see them? The moon was fairly bright overhead. Fear kept her half breathless and utterly motionless as she waited to see what was going to happen.

A rush of intense relief shuddered through her when his gaze tracked past where they were hidden. He gazed around for another long minute and then continued on his way.

She felt the sigh of relief from Luke on the back of her neck. Thank God Pierre hadn't decided to come and investigate the source of the loud sound.

They continued to follow Pierre. He wound up at the same area. He uncovered the boat, got into it and then disappeared in the darkness.

Luke remained hidden with her and thankfully didn't speak as they didn't know the exact location of the gatorhunter. She was still shaken up by the close call they had had.

If Pierre found them spying on him, what would he

do? Would he just scream and yell at them? Or would he try to kill them? There was no way of knowing and in any case, she didn't want to find out.

This time, Pierre was only gone about an hour. He returned to the shore, unloaded the boat and hid it, and then began the trek back to his shanty. Apparently, the fish and gators hadn't cooperated with him tonight because he'd come back empty-handed.

Once he was back in his shanty, she and Luke returned to her place. When they got inside, she collapsed on the sofa and drew several long, deep breaths.

Luke sank down next to her. "God, I'm so sorry," he said.

She immediately knew what he was apologizing for. "There's no need for you to apologize. It could just have easily been me who stepped on the branch and snapped it."

"Damn, it was so loud and I was sure Pierre was going to find us."

"All's well that ends well, right?" She drew another deep breath and felt herself finally relaxing. "Do you want to eat something?"

"No, thanks. I always eat—"

"I know, you always eat around six o'clock each night." She looked at him curiously. "What would happen if you ate at seven or midnight? Would you suddenly go mad and bay at the moon?"

He laughed. "No, nothing like that." He sobered thoughtfully. "I'm the first one to admit that I'm tied to my schedules and routines. Rationally, I know it's baggage from my childhood. But I'm working on it. After all, I did dance in the rain with you."

She smiled at him. "Yes, you did." Her head filled with the memory of being held in his strong arms and dancing as the rain came down to caress them. Then he'd kissed her and she wanted him to kiss her again right in this moment.

She leaned toward him as their gazes remained locked. He angled his body to her and a hot anticipation simmered inside her. Closer and closer he came toward her and then he suddenly snapped back and straightened up.

"I'll just get out of here and head home," he said as he rose from the sofa.

Disappointed, she got up as well. She'd been so sure he was going to kiss her again, but it hadn't happened. She walked with him to the front door.

"Good night, Dominique," he said as he opened her door. "I'll see you tomorrow night."

"Good night, Luke." As he walked out into the night, she closed and locked her door behind him.

She could have sworn he'd wanted to kiss her. She had seen a flame of desire in the depths of his green eyes. What had stopped him? Had she misread the desire? With a deep sigh, she turned off all the lanterns in the shanty except one, and that one she carried into her bedroom.

She'd thought she was hungry, but she decided just to go to bed instead. It was late and she was on duty at the café for breakfast the next morning.

It wasn't long before she was in bed and asleep, and having dreams once again of dancing with and kissing Luke. Her alarm blared its wake-up call early the next morning and she got out of bed, dressed and got ready to go.

As she drove into work, she couldn't help but think about that moment when she'd thought Luke was going to kiss her again. There was no question that she was physically drawn to him and she believed he was to her, too. She saw it in his eyes when he gazed at her and felt it in his very touch.

Was she mistaken? She didn't believe so. She truly believed his desire for her matched her desire for him. Would it be so awful if they acted on it and slept together?

She smiled to herself and wondered where on his schedule making love fit in? The man couldn't even adjust the time he ate, for crying out loud. And that reminded her of why he would never have a place in her future.

If they did fall in bed together, it wouldn't be making love. Rather, it would just be an act of physical desire. Passion could come without love, right?

As she pulled up and parked behind the café, she shoved all thoughts of Luke and passion out of her head. It was time to go in and serve the good people of Dark Waters.

"Hey, girl, long time no talk," Sunny said as Dominique walked into the break room.

"I know. I've just really been busy lately," Dominique replied.

"Yeah, busy with the handsome Officer Madison. What is going on between you and Luke?" Sunny gazed at her with open curiosity.

Dominique opened a locker and put her purse inside before replying. "Luke and I are just friends. He's…uh… helping me out with a personal problem."

Sunny's gaze turned sardonic. "It sure didn't look like just friends when the two of you had lunch together the other day. That man looked at you like he wanted to eat you up."

Dominique laughed. "He was probably looking at me as if I was an alien being. The two of us are very different."

Sunny shook her head. "Nope, that wasn't it, but obviously you're being tight-lipped about your relationship with him. I get it if you're not wanting to share it with me right now."

"Sunny, I promise you there is nothing to share and you know I'd tell you if there was anything," Dominique said with a small laugh. She slammed the locker and pocketed the key. "Now, it's time to get to work."

Minutes later, Dominique was taking orders and delivering food to the people in her section. There were several of her regulars there, including Burt and Austin.

"Hey, Jacob. What can I get for you this morning?" she said, greeting another one of her regulars. Jacob Benoit was a fisherman. He was single and rather attractive, and often blatantly flirted with Dominique.

"I'll take a serving of you on a silver platter," he replied with a bright twinkle in his dark eyes.

"Sorry, Jacob, unfortunately we are all out of our silver platters this morning," she replied.

"Damn," he replied with a grin. "Then I guess just give me my regular number two breakfast special. Hopefully, tomorrow morning there will be some silver platters in the house."

She laughed. "We'll have to see about that."

"Maybe you could save one for me," he replied.

"Sorry again, but we aren't allowed to save the silver platters."

"Oh, Dominique, you're absolutely breaking my heart," he said with mock melancholy.

She laughed once again. "I'm sure eating your breakfast will heal it right up. I'll be right back with your food."

She was still smiling as she moved away from his table. She had to admit, she enjoyed some of the teasing and flirting as long as it didn't go too far and get creepy. It was all in good fun.

She also enjoyed it when the café was busy. Although it kept her on her feet, running from the pass where she picked up the food and then carrying it to tables to be served, it also made the time go very quickly.

Before she knew it, it was three o'clock and her day at work was finished. She couldn't wait to get home and take a shower. She always felt like she smelled of fried onions when she left work. Since it was a hot day with the sun bright overhead, she knew the rainwater she showered in would be nice and warm.

It didn't take her long to arrive at the swamp's entrance. She got out of her car and then began the walk in toward her shanty. As she walked, her thoughts were a jumble with Luke at the forefront.

How long would he be willing to continue backing her up at night when she shadowed Pierre? He'd mentioned that he was on vacation. When his vacation time was over, would he still continue the nightly quests with her? More concerning was without his presence as backup, would she be willing to do it all alone?

All of a sudden, from behind her a burlap bag fell over her head. She instantly stiffened as abject fear torched through her. What? Dear God, what was happening? She couldn't see and danger screamed in her head.

The person behind her attempted to pull the large bag farther down her body and she knew if he managed to do that, then she would either be dead or she would never be seen again.

Luke pushed back in his recliner. The plan was to get a short nap in before meeting Dominique later that night. It was just after three so he should be able to sleep for about an hour and a half, and then get up and fix himself some dinner.

He thought about the brief conversation he'd had with Dominique about his meal times. Logically, he knew the world wouldn't explode if he ate at a different time. But emotionally it was difficult to give up on the schedules that had made him feel safe and in control after his tumultuous childhood.

He closed his eyes and tried to empty his mind as he sought sleep. But a vision of Dominique danced through his brain. She had wanted him to kiss her the night before.

She had leaned toward him, her lips parted in open invitation as her scent eddied in his head. Damn, he had wanted to kiss her again but was now thankful that he'd managed to keep his control. Kissing Dominique was dangerous because he knew it would only make him want to kiss her again…and again. Even though it would be wonderful, it wasn't appropriate for their relationship as friends.

He had just drifted off when his phone rang. He grabbed it from the end table next to him. "Madison," he answered.

"Luke…it's…it's me. I… I need you to come to my shanty." Her voice was shaky and it sounded like she was crying.

"Dominique, what's wrong?" he asked, all lingering vestiges of sleep falling away.

"Please…just come here as soon as you can," she replied and then hung up.

He jumped up from the chair and shoved his cell phone into his back pocket. He then hurried into the kitchen where he strapped on his shoulder holster, grabbed his keys and then raced out of his apartment.

He didn't know what was going on, but he had never heard her sound the way she had. It was obvious something had tremendously upset her and all he wanted to do was get to her as quickly as possible.

He drove as fast as he could, given the other traffic on the road. What on earth had happened to her? He couldn't imagine and he refused to allow his imagination to roam free. He just needed to get to her as soon as possible and find out what was going on.

It didn't take him long to reach the swamp's entrance, where he jumped out of his car and headed in. He moved quickly along the paths that were now fairly familiar to him.

It seemed like it took him forever but he finally reached her bridge and raced across it to her front door. "Dominique, it's me," he called out.

He heard her unlock the door and then it opened and she half collapsed into his arms. Her sobs tore at his heart as he held her tight for several long moments. At least she didn't appear physically hurt.

He moved her farther inside and then closed the door behind them and led her to the sofa. She remained clinging to him as she continued to weep.

"Hey, hey," he said softly as he caressed her up and down her back in an effort to comfort her. He gazed around the room to see if anything looked amiss. But the room was as neat and tidy as it always was. "What's happened? Tell me what's going on, Dominique."

She finally released her hold on him and sank down on the sofa. He sat next to her as she drew several deep breaths in an obvious effort to get her tears under control.

"I—I was walking back here a-after work," she began. Although the sobs had finally stopped, tears still oozed from her eyes. "I wasn't paying a-attention. Th-that was my mistake because I never heard him come up behind me."

Her words instantly made all of Luke's muscles tense and a chill walked up his spine. He reached for her hand and she grasped his tightly, as if it was a lifeline. She released a deep, shaky breath and stared down at the coffee table as she continued to speak.

"He came up behind me and pulled what felt and smelled like a burlap bag over my head. Oh Luke, I was so terrified. For a moment I just froze. As he tried to pull the big bag down farther on my body, I fumbled in my purse and managed to grab my knife. I started stabbing out all around. I guess he didn't expect me to have any kind of weapon."

The words now tumbled from her, nearly tripping over each other as she continued to relay what had happened to her. Her fingers squeezed together with his even tighter as tears once again filled her eyes.

"I… I think I managed to stab him somewhere because he let out a low grunt. I kicked and stabbed and tried desperately to get the bag off of me. I fought as hard as I could and then I heard him running away. I pulled the bag off my head and tried to get a look at who it was, but he was already gone."

She released his hand and instead swiped at her tears, then finally gazed at him. The fear was still in the depths of her eyes and her lips trembled slightly. "I don't know if he wanted to rape me, kill me or kidnap me."

He reached out and gently drew a thumb across her cheeks to wipe away the last of her tears. His heart still thundered in his chest with fear for her. "Thank God you managed to fight him off, Dominique," he said. "And now I need to call Daniel. We need to make an official police report of this."

She nodded and he pulled his phone from his pocket to

make the call. Dominique looked so small, so fragile half curled up in the corner of the sofa. All he really wanted to do was hold her and comfort her until the residual fear was gone from her beautiful eyes.

Once he made the call to Daniel, he did just that. He reached out and pulled her into his embrace. She came willingly into his arms. They didn't speak. He just held her and occasionally he felt a small shiver go through her body.

She finally moved out of his arms and leaned back against the sofa. "I just can't believe this happened to me."

"Thank God you managed to get your knife out of your purse," he replied.

"If I hadn't, he would have had me." She wrapped her arms around herself, and once again looked small and vulnerable. She sat there for a long moment and then got up. "I'm going to go change out of my work clothes. I'll be right back."

As she left the living room and disappeared into her bedroom, Luke leaned back and released a deep sigh. Who had attacked her? It had to have been whoever had left her the note. Unfortunately, Clay had been unable to pull any prints from it.

You will belong to me.

The words now took on a far more ominous meaning. Whoever had written the note had been the man who had attacked her, Luke was sure of that. It had been a very bold move considering it had taken place in the middle of the afternoon and other people could have been around.

However, surely if anyone had seen her being attacked, the person would have come to help her. The fact that nobody had come to her aid let him know there were probably no witnesses to the assault.

She came back into the living room, now clad in a housedress that was dark with light blue flowers. It appeared there were snaps that ran from the neckline to the bottom of the garment. It skimmed her body and she looked beautiful and casual in it, except for her eyes. They remained dark and haunted with fear.

"Feel better?" he asked.

She nodded and returned to the sofa. At that moment there was a knock on the door. "I'll get it," Luke said and got up. He assumed it was Daniel and he was right. Clay was with him, along with Roger Teasdale, another day cop.

They all came inside where Daniel sat in the recliner facing Dominique on the sofa and the other two men stood on either side of him.

"Hi, Dominique," he greeted her softly. "Are you okay?"

"As okay as I can be," she replied.

"Luke told me a little bit of what was going on, but I want you to tell me exactly what happened," Daniel said as he pulled a notepad from his pocket.

As she once again relayed the afternoon event, Luke's muscles tensed up all over again. He wanted to find the man and beat the hell out of him for touching her…for frightening her so badly. He wanted the man in jail for what he'd done to her.

Once she was finished telling Daniel what had happened, Daniel began to ask her questions. "You didn't see him at all?"

She shook her head. "By the time I got free of the bag over my head, he was gone."

"Did you smell anything? Maybe cologne or something else?" Daniel asked. She paused for a long moment and then shook her head.

"All I smelled was the burlap of the bag," she replied.

"Well, it's obvious the note that was left for you is connected to this. I would guess he intended to kidnap you," Daniel said. His words shot a new fear for her through Luke.

Daniel continued to question her, including asking her where, in the swamp, this encounter had taken place. Once he had a good idea of that, he sent Clay and Roger out to see if they could find anything that might help them identify the perp. If they were lucky, he might have dropped something that would give them some clarity.

Once they left, Daniel continued questioning Dominique. "I want you to think of any man who has been giving you attention lately. Not only in your personal life, but in your work life as well."

"There's nobody in my personal life except Luke," she replied.

"What about at the café?"

She frowned. "I've got three regulars who instantly come to mind. They are flirty with me, but it's all in good fun. I can't imagine any of them being responsible for this."

"Names?" Daniel asked.

Another frown tugged across her forehead. "There's Burt Stanfield. Second is Austin Colbert and the third is Jacob Benoit. They're all regulars of mine and they all flirt with me, but it's nothing deep and I still just can't imagine one of them attacked me this afternoon."

Daniel wrote the names down. "The three of them are a good place to start my investigation. We'll check out their alibis for the afternoon and see what we come up with." He looked up at her at her once again. "What about old boyfriends? Who was the last person you dated?"

"Oliver LeBoeuf, but that was almost a year ago," she replied.

"Who broke up with whom?" Daniel asked.

"I broke things off with him, but we parted on a friendly basis. I can't imagine him being behind all this, either," she protested. "This is all my fault," she added miserably, the words surprising Luke.

"How on earth could it have been your fault?" he asked incredulously.

"I should have been more aware. I should have heard him come up behind me long before he was close enough to put a burlap bag over my head. But I was into my own head and distracted. Had I been paying more attention this probably wouldn't have happened."

"That's not true," Luke said, jumping to her defense. "No way should you take on any responsibility for what happened to you."

"And I definitely agree with Luke," Daniel added. "Nobody is responsible for the attack on you except the perpetrator, and I promise you I'm going to do everything in my power to find out who that is as quickly as possible."

Dominique opened her mouth as if to say something, but then she grasped the locket that Luke now knew from one of their previous conversations held some of her mother's ashes, and bit her bottom lip.

Luke could guess what she wanted to say. Daniel had promised the very same thing concerning her mother's murder and here it was a little over two months later with nobody in jail for the crime.

At that moment, the door opened and Clay and Roger returned. Clay carried with him a large burlap bag. "We found it right in the area where Dominique told us she'd been attacked."

"Did you find anything else around that area?" Daniel asked.

"No, nothing more," Roger replied.

"And we checked the area very thoroughly," Clay added.

"Get the burlap sack into an evidence bag," Daniel said with a frown. "I don't know how well burlap retains fingerprints but hopefully you can go over it to see what you can find," he said to Clay.

"I doubt you'll find anything," Luke said. "We didn't find any prints on the note that was left so I would imagine the person wore gloves."

"You're probably right, but we'll check it out anyway," Daniel replied. "And the first person I intend to talk to is Jacob Benoit. Fishermen often use burlap bags to keep their fish in." He stood and Luke did the same while Dominique remained curled in the corner of the sofa.

"Dominique, I'm so sorry this happened to you," Daniel said sympathetically. "I'll be in touch, and if you think of anything that might help us identify who did this to you, then don't hesitate to tell Luke or call me."

"I will," she replied.

"I'll be in touch as soon as I have information or more questions for you," Daniel said.

Luke walked with him and the other officers to the front door. "I'll also be in touch," Luke replied. The men all said goodbye and then they left.

Luke relocked the door and then turned back to Dominique. At least some of the color had returned to her cheeks and she didn't look quite as frightened as she had when he'd first arrived.

He sank back down next to her and she moved closer to him. "How are you doing?" he asked gently.

"A little better now, although I still can't believe it all happened. He tried to kidnap me," she said softly. She gazed into his eyes. The gaze was so intense he felt as if she was looking into the very depths of his soul. "Luke, will you hold me again?" she asked.

"Of course," he replied. He pulled her back into his arms and she buried her face in his shoulder as her arms wrapped around his neck.

Her heart beat against his own and the scent of her eddied in his head. He was there to comfort her, but he couldn't help how the closeness to her half dizzied his senses.

They remained that way for several long moments and then she raised her head and once again gazed at him. Her eyes held a winsome plea. "Kiss me, Luke. Please, I want… I need you to kiss me."

He shouldn't. It wasn't right. The rational thoughts tried to find purchase in his brain, but it was impossible with the flames he saw in the very depths of her eyes. It was impossible with her luscious, full lips so close to his.

He knew her lips would be sinfully soft, and even knowing it was wrong, even knowing he would probably regret it later, he couldn't fight against his own desire to taste her lips.

She was a fever that burned hot, a rush inside his blood. He'd sworn he wasn't going to kiss her again, but here he was…about to kiss her once again.

Chapter Seven

Dominique's heart fluttered and a sweet desire filled her as Luke's mouth took hers. The kiss filled her with a warmth that sought out and banished all the cold places the attack had created inside her.

She opened her mouth to his and their tongues swirled together in a hot dance of desire. He smelled so good and his arms around her felt so familiar and so…safe.

However, it wasn't safety she was looking for from him at the moment. She tasted his passion for her and it made her feel wonderfully alive as it stirred a wealth of desire for him inside her.

She'd never loved kissing a man as much as she loved kissing Luke. His lips didn't pressure, rather they cajoled a response. And respond she did.

Her heart beat fast and furiously and she quickly became half breathless. She realized at that moment she wanted far more than a kiss from him. She wanted to explore completely the physical attraction that burned bright inside her.

She felt as if she'd desired him from the first moment he had shown up on her doorstep to act as her bodyguard. Now that desire was completely out of control and all she could think about was Luke and how much she wanted him.

The kiss finally ended. He was as breathless as she. She took his hand in hers and stood. "Luke, come to my bedroom and make love with me."

"That's probably not a good idea," he said, his voice deeper than usual.

"Why? Don't you want me?" She gazed into his beautiful eyes and was assured by the desire she saw lighting the green depths. He looked so handsome in his jeans and a mint-green button-up shirt, but she was eager to see him naked and she desperately wanted to have him in bed with her.

"That's not the point," he replied. "You've had a bad scare and—"

"And nothing," she said, interrupting him. "Luke, I wanted you last night and the night before that. This has nothing to do with the attack. This is just me wanting you. Come into my bedroom with me, Luke. Come and make love with me." She gave his hand a soft tug, thrilled when he finally stood.

She led him into her bedroom where she turned on the lantern next to the bed. As she turned to face him, he immediately drew her back into his arms for another kiss. She wrapped her arms around his neck and leaned into him as his arms tightened around her. She leaned close enough to him that she felt his arousal against her.

Raw, hot desire roared through her as his hands drew sensual circles on her back. All she could think about was Luke and how much she wanted him.

They kissed for only a moment and then she pulled her hands from around his neck and instead began to unbutton his shirt. He stood perfectly still, his eyes smoldering as she slowly worked the buttons.

As she unfastened each one, she kissed the warm, bare skin that was exposed. As she worked down his chest, his breathing quickened and he released a low moan.

"Dominique, you're driving me absolutely crazy," he half growled.

She smiled up at him. "That's the whole point." She shoved his shirt off his shoulders and it fell to the floor behind them. Oh, he had a glorious chest, broad and firmly muscled.

He kicked off his loafers as she unbuttoned the fly on his jeans. "Take them off, Luke," she whispered urgently.

She didn't have to ask twice. As he unzipped them then pulled them and his socks off, she turned down the spread, exposing pale pink sheets.

When she gazed at him again, he was clad only in a pair of navy-blue boxers. Her breath caught in her throat at the sight of his beautiful body. Rather than being an overly muscular, bulked-up man, Luke had the kind of wiry build she'd always found attractive on a man.

As he stared at her, his eyes lit with green flames of want, she began to unsnap the housedress she'd thrown on earlier. With each snap she opened, the flames in his eyes grew more intense.

She wore no bra beneath, so once the housedress was open, she was clad only in a pair of wispy pink panties. She shrugged the dress off her shoulders and it joined his shirt and jeans on the floor.

"You are so beautiful," he half whispered.

"So are you," she replied. She slid beneath the sheet on the bed and beckoned him to join her there. He got in next to her and immediately sought her mouth again with his. As they kissed, their legs tangled together. She loved the feel of his strong, naked legs against hers.

For a few minutes their bodies remained close and the tactile pleasure of his bare skin against hers felt wonderful. His chest was so broad against her own and she could feel their hearts beating together in unison.

He shifted positions so he had a free hand to stroke down her body. He caressed first one breast and then the other, toying with each of her hardened nipples. He then lowered his head and captured one of the nipples in his mouth.

"Oh yes," she said on a moan as the pleasure shot an electrical fire from her nipples to the very center of her. He teased and licked first one and then the other until she was half mad with want.

His hand began to move lower, slowly trailing fingers down her abdomen and to the waistband of her panties. He slid his fingers back and forth across the panties' band, tormenting her as her desire for him raged completely out of control.

She reached down and removed the only barrier other than his boxers keeping them apart. She threw the panties to the floor and then she was back in his arms. This time as he slid his hand back down, there was nothing to stop him from touching her moist center.

She moaned and raised her hips to meet his intimate touch. His fingers danced against her. Her muscles tightened as she began to climb up and up to a place of pleasure she'd never been before.

She clung to his shoulders as she moved her hips more frantically, rising to heights that had her gasping with need. And then she was there, spiraling down with the force of the orgasm that shuddered through her.

As soon as she was able, she reached out to him and caressed down his chest. But he stopped her. “I don’t need any more foreplay,” he said, his eyes glowing with his desire.

He reached down and took off his boxers, then rolled her onto her back and positioned himself between her thighs. He bent down and took her mouth in a gentle kiss as he slowly eased into her.

Powerful and intense, the sensations that rushed through her were beyond wonderful. He began to pump in and out of her and thought was impossible. There was only her and Luke and these breathtaking moments.

He moaned and she grabbed hold of his buttocks. “Faster, Luke. Faster,” she said. He quickened his pace and before long they became frantic, panting as they moved together.

Once again, she felt the tension building inside her, taking her to an unsustainable high. She cried out his name as her climax crashed over her and a moment later, he stiffened against her and moaned with his own release. When it was over, he collapsed on his back next to her, both of them wordless as they fought to find a more normal breathing.

Finally, he raised himself up on one elbow and gazed at her with a soft smile. He moved a strand of her hair away from her face. “That was amazing,” he said.

“It was beyond amazing,” she replied. It had been intense and passionate and more incredible than she had ever imagined. “Can you stay the rest of the evening with me?”

“Of course,” he replied. “I would have been here anyway, but I think for tonight we shouldn’t go out to follow Pierre.”

She released a tremulous sigh. "I agree. I just need some time to process and get over the attack."

He leaned down and kissed her gently on the forehead. "I'm just so sorry that happened to you. Let's hope Daniel can get us some answers very soon."

"Enough about that."

He stared at her, this time his gaze obviously curious. "Dominique, what exactly are we doing?"

"Nothing serious, so don't get weird on me, Luke," she replied. "Now, you can use the bathroom first."

"Okay." He slid out of the bed and grabbed his clothes from the floor, then left the bedroom.

She looked over to the window where twilight displayed itself in shades of dark purples and grays. The day was nearly done. She had no desire to go out into the swamp tonight. She just wanted to spend more time with Luke.

"The bathroom is all yours," he said from the doorway. "I'll just meet you in the living room."

She got out of bed, grabbed her housedress and a clean pair of panties, and then headed into the bathroom. Once there she looked at herself in the mirror. She'd wanted to make love with Luke and now she had. She'd wondered what kind of a lover he'd be and now she knew.

At times he'd been gentle but he'd also been masterful and giving and the whole thing had been utterly magical. She'd assumed once her curiosity about him as a lover had been sated then that would be the end of it. But to her surprise, she wanted him again…and again. It had nothing to do with love, but everything to do with the crazy, wild desire she felt for him.

She turned away from the mirror, cleaned herself up

and then redressed and left the bathroom. He was seated on the sofa and he smiled at her as she entered the room.

"I just thought of something," she said.

"What's that?" he asked curiously.

"You missed your six o'clock dinner. How about I fry up some bacon and make some eggs and toast?"

He grinned. "Even though I'm off my schedule, that sounds really good."

"Why don't you come into the kitchen and talk to me while I cook?"

"With pleasure." He got up from the sofa and followed her into the kitchen. She gestured for him to sit at the table. "I'll be right back," she said and then went out the back door to start her generator.

For just a moment she stood at the railing and stared into the dark water beneath her. The last gasp of twilight played in the water, reflecting the colors of a dying day.

Who had attacked her? A chill walked up her spine as she thought about the unexpected assault. She wondered why they had tried to kidnap her. And more importantly, would they try again?

They ate eggs and bacon and small-talked through the meal. Luke still couldn't believe what had happened between them. Making love with Dominique had been the most powerful experience he'd ever had. Even now, as he gazed at her across her small kitchen table, he wanted her again.

He'd loved the feel and taste of her soft skin. It could become an addiction if he allowed it. She'd been so passionate and the whole experience had been mind-blowing.

"Dominique, everything happened so fast between

us, we didn't even use birth control," he said once they were finished eating and she was cleaning up the dishes.

She turned from the sink to look at him. "It's okay. I'm on birth control pills and I haven't been with anyone for a long time."

"Same for me," he said. "Except the birth control pills part. You do realize we shouldn't have fallen into bed together," he added.

"Why not? We're both consenting adults and we wanted each other. We certainly didn't hurt anyone by acting on our desire for each other."

"Yes, but I don't want things to get confusing for us. I don't want to complicate a relationship that I enjoy," he replied.

"Luke, you're taking things way too seriously," she said. She turned back around to the sink.

He supposed he was getting weird about it. He wished he could be as nonchalant as she was, but he took making love with a woman seriously. He sipped his coffee in silence while she finished up with the dishes. But he wasn't in love with her. He couldn't be.

They went back into the living room where she turned on lanterns and then sank down next to him on the sofa. "Do you work tomorrow?" he asked.

"I do. I'm on breakfast duty." Her beautiful chocolate eyes appeared to darken. "And there's always a possibility a few of my regulars might come in. Sometimes they're there for lunch and sometimes they come in for breakfast."

"Keep in mind, right now they're just men Daniel will investigate, but that doesn't mean any of them are guilty."

"Then who is?"

"I wish I could answer that for you," he replied intensely. “If I knew who it was, I’d beat the hell out of him for what he did to you.”

She grinned at him. “You’d do that for me?”

“In a short minute,” he replied.

She sighed. “I’ll just be glad if Daniel gets whoever it is behind bars.”

“He will,” Luke replied, confident in his friend’s skills as a lawman.

“He hasn’t done so well in my mother’s murder investigation,” she replied.

“That’s a different animal altogether. Knowing somebody is guilty and having the evidence to prove it are two different things. And it wasn’t just Daniel investigating your mother’s murder—it was me, too.”

“Do you think it will ever be solved?” she asked. Her gaze held his intently.

“Oh, I think it’s already solved,” he replied.

“Okay, wrong question…do you think Pierre will ever be arrested?”

He grinned at her. “Well, if you have anything to do with it, definitely.”

“Now, you’re making fun of me,” she said, and her lower lip jutted out in a mock pout.

He laughed. “No, I swear I’m not, but I still have little faith that at some point in time Pierre will dig up your mother’s missing book and we’ll catch him.”

“It could happen.”

He laughed again. “Yes, it could happen, and that’s why I’m here with you.”

“Speaking of being here for me. Want to spend the night? We could be snuggle buddies.”

Although her tone was light, there was something in

her gaze that told him she wasn't quite ready to be alone yet. "I love snuggling," he replied.

"Then you'll stay?" This time her tone was less casual.

"I'll stay." It would be another blunder in the long list of mistakes he'd already made today.

"Thank you," she replied, her gratitude rife in her tone. "And speaking of bedtime, I should probably head to bed now since I have to get up so early in the morning."

"Yeah, I'm tired, too," he admitted. It had been a day of intense emotions, both good and bad.

She stood and he also got up. She doused all the lit lanterns in the room. The lantern in the bedroom made it easy for them to find their way. She grabbed a pink night-gown from one of her drawers and then disappeared once again into the bathroom.

Luke stripped down to his boxers and then got into bed. He was happy to snuggle with her if that's what she needed, but he had no intention of repeating what they had shared in bed earlier. That had definitely been a blunder.

She came back into the room, looking beautiful in the lantern's soft light. The pink color of the nightgown was perfect against her dark hair and skin tone. Her hair was loose and spilled down her back like a waterfall of shiny silk.

"I wasn't sure which side of the bed you wanted," he said. She slid in next to him.

"This is perfect." She was next to the nightstand where she placed his phone and hers. "I've got my alarm set for five. I hate to wake you up so early. If you can, feel free to stay here and sleep longer when I leave for work."

"Nah, I'll get up with you and follow you into work and then I'll force you to wait on me by sitting in your section. I'll complain about the food and service and then I'll leave you a five percent tip."

She laughed. "You won't do that," she replied.

"No, I won't complain no matter how bad the service is," he said, making her laugh once again.

"Are you ready for the light to go off?" she asked once the laughter had passed.

"Whenever you are," he said.

She reached out and turned off the lantern on the nightstand. He then pulled her into him, spooning around her back while she snuggled into him.

Torture. It was sheer torture to have her so close against him. Her scent filled his head as her bottom wiggled into him. He tightened his arm around her, wanting her to feel as safe as possible as she fell asleep.

Meanwhile, he prayed sleep would come quickly to him as he fought against another wave of desire. "Luke?"

"Yes?"

"Thank you," she said softly.

"No need to thank me," he replied. What she needed from him now was a sense of safety after the assault, and that thought doused his desire. "Good night, Dominique."

"Good night, Luke."

He knew the moment she fell asleep. Her body went completely limp against his and her breathing became slow and rhythmic. Unfortunately, sleep was elusive for him.

His mind whirled with everything that had happened from the moment he'd gotten the frantic phone call from her until now. It had been such a wild day.

He hoped that tomorrow she wouldn't regret sleeping with him, and he hoped that she wouldn't realize she'd made an impulsive jump into his arms because of the terrifying incident she'd suffered earlier.

It had been a very long time since he'd cuddled a woman in sleep. In his last relationship, the woman had hated being touched at night. She stayed on her side of the bed and he had stayed on his. That had been over a year ago and since that time he hadn't dated or tried to cuddle with anyone.

He must have fallen asleep as he awakened to the sound of raucous loud music coming from Dominique's phone. To his surprise, they were still in the position they had been in when they'd fallen asleep.

She stirred and he removed his arm from around her and moved away from her as she reached out to grab her phone. The music stopped and she let out a small groan. "Is it time to get up already?"

"Your phone says it is," he replied.

She sat up and turned on the lantern against the darkness in the room. At five in the morning, there was no sign of the morning sun. "If you want to, go back to sleep," she said as she got out of bed.

"Now that I'm awake, I'll just get up and get dressed," he replied.

"Why don't you go ahead and get in the bathroom while I'm getting my clothes together," she replied. As she turned on another lantern on top of the dresser, he slid out of the bed, grabbed his clothes and then headed to the bathroom.

He should have time to get home, take a shower and then head to the café for breakfast. Hopefully all of Dominique's regulars would show up this morning and he could get a good look at them all.

You will belong to me. As he thought of the note she'd

received along with the attack on her, his biggest fear right now was that another attack would come—only this time the perp would be successful.

He awakened early, a wild disappointment still raging through him. He should have been able to take her yesterday. It had been so perfect. She'd been alone on the narrow path and hadn't heard him creeping up behind her.

When he'd managed to get the bag over her head, he'd been so sure of his success. He hadn't counted on her having a knife and he also hadn't counted on how hard she would fight against him. It had been like trying to contain a hellcat in a paper bag.

He sat at his kitchen table, the eggs he'd made himself for breakfast growing cold as he stared out the nearby window and thought about her.

Dominique Santori. Her very name sang in his heart. She was the woman of his dreams and all he could think about was getting her into his house where he could enjoy her company forever. She would fill up the dark, lonely hours that had become his life.

He gazed down at the nick in his skin. The little knife cut was now covered with a small bandage and would heal up fairly quickly. But it was a reminder of his failure.

He got up from the table and dumped his eggs in the trash and then went down the hallway to the door that led into the room he'd prepared especially for her.

The walls had been soundproofed and were painted an eggshell beige. The twin bed was covered in a pink, frilly bedspread that nearly hid the ropes that fell to the floor on either side. He'd have to tie her down until she became obedient and understood that she was where she belonged.

He could just imagine her sitting at the vanity table

in front of the aluminum mirror and brushing her long, beautiful hair. Then he would take his turn and brush through the silky strands.

The room also had a small table with two chairs. They would eat their meals there until the time came when he could trust her outside of this room. There was also an en suite bathroom for her to use.

He believed he'd thought of everything. There was nothing sharp in the room that she could use as a weapon and he had everything he needed for her, everything that would keep her here forever.

Oh, it was going to be so wonderful. He closed the door and returned to sit at the kitchen table. His life wouldn't be complete until he had her in it.

And he would get her. She'd gotten away from him yesterday, but the next time he went after her, he would be better prepared. Oh yes…his excitement made him half dizzy. Sweet anticipation roared through him. Soon… very, very soon, she would be his.

Chapter Eight

Waking up in Luke's arms had been wonderful. As Dominique drove to the café the next morning, she still felt the warmth of his body close to hers and his arm wrapped around her waist. She'd felt so safe…so protected and warm.

The kidnapping attempt that had occurred the day before now seemed oddly distant, as if it had taken place days ago. She knew it was because of so many things that had happened after the attack.

Making love with Luke and having him next to her all night long had taken away the rough edges of fear that the assault had left behind.

However, Luke couldn't be there all the time. She had to be there for herself, and that meant staying vigilante. She had to watch her surroundings and couldn't allow any mind lapses to make her an easy target again in the future.

As she parked behind the café, a nervous energy fluttered through her as she thought about waiting on her regulars. Was one of them responsible for the kidnapping attempt? Beneath the flirty words and easy smiles, did one of them have some sort of a dangerous obsession for her?

You will belong to me.

The words now definitely had an ominous meaning. Was it possible that one of the men she served breakfast to had written it? For the first time she could ever remember, she was dreading going in to work.

However, it was time she get her butt inside. She looked all around the parking lot before getting out of her car, and then she hurried in through the back door.

Things were wonderfully normal as she walked into the warm kitchen that smelled of frying onions and eggs, of bacon and ham and other breakfast items. Annie greeted her, as did Ed Slavoie, Annie's right-hand man, and several other members of the staff.

She walked into the break room where Cindy Lawson and Glenda Wright, two other waitresses, were getting ready to clock in. Sunny wasn't working this morning, but Dominique was friendly with the other two waitresses. There were three more waitresses scheduled to work and they should be rolling in at any time.

Once again, she dreaded seeing her regulars today. How would they all react when Daniel spoke with them? Would they be angry with her for giving him their names? Appalled that she would believe any one of them could be behind the attack on her?

By seven o'clock, the café was filling up and Dominique and the others were busy taking orders and running food. By eight o'clock, Luke walked in, looking handsome as the devil in a pair of jeans and a blue polo shirt that emphasized his broad shoulders.

His presence immediately made her feel less jittery about seeing her regulars when they came in. Luke offered her a huge grin as he sat in one of the two-tops in her section.

She walked over to the table to take his order. "Oh,

you again," she said teasingly. "Could you please tip me more than your usual five percent today? My babies are hungry and they all need new shoes."

He laughed. "We'll see," he replied. "Of course, it will depend solely on the service I receive."

"Then I'll see if I can get it right today," she replied.

The twinkling in his eyes dimmed a bit. "Anyone interesting in here?"

"Not yet." She knew he was referring to the three men she'd told Daniel about. "They should show up any minute now."

"When they do, point them out to me and let me know who is who."

She nodded. "Okay, now what can I get you to eat?"

"I'll take a number four special," he replied.

She raised a brow. The number four was the largest breakfast on the menu. "A bit hungry this morning?"

Once again, the twinkle was back in his eyes. "Yeah, I worked up quite an appetite yesterday afternoon."

She laughed. "Okay, a number four it is. Coffee?"

"Definitely."

"I'll be right back with that." She left his table, her heart warmed by the brief interaction with him. She served his coffee and then a few minutes later returned with his large platter of food.

By that time Burt had come in and had taken a seat in her section. She walked back by Luke's table. "Burt Stanfield," she said softly and then headed toward him. She knew Luke probably knew Burt since he worked for the city.

"Good morning, doll," Burt said in greeting.

"How are you doing this morning?" she asked him with what she hoped looked like her usual, friendly smile.

"I'm doing just fine," he replied. "And speaking of fine…you look mighty fine this morning."

"Thank you, Burt. Now, what can I get you?"

"I'll take the number two special with coffee."

"I'll be right back with your coffee," she said.

She wondered if he'd picked up on the fact that she really didn't want their usual flirty banter this morning. She served his coffee and then a few minutes later returned with his food order.

"Everything okay this morning, Dominique?" he asked her. So, he had sensed the difference in her.

"Everything is just fine, Burt," she replied with what she hoped was a reassuring smile. "I've just been really busy this morning."

"Then don't let me hold you up," he replied.

"Thanks, Burt, I'll check in with you a little later," she said and then left his table.

About fifteen minutes later Austin came in and the scene repeated itself. She walked by Luke's table and let him know who Austin was and then went to wait on him.

Luke stayed until just after ten. The only regular who didn't come in was Jacob Benoit, who she usually saw in the afternoons. Once Luke left, she felt oddly bereft.

Thankfully, the café stayed busy until almost eleven and then there was a lull. The breakfast crowd had left and the lunch crowd hadn't come in yet.

Annie sent her on break and this time—rather than stepping outside—she sat in the break room and played on her phone and tried not to think about what was going on in her life.

Still, her thoughts couldn't help but go back to the kidnapping attempt. How close was danger now? Was the person right now someplace plotting and thinking about how to get her?

Given the note and the attack, she was sure the person wouldn't just give up and go away. So, from what direction would danger come at her again? She could only wait and hope that she would survive whatever might happen.

It was just after noon when Luke pulled up behind the police station and parked. He was eager to check in with Daniel and let him know his impressions of the two men he'd seen at the café.

He found his boss in his office. "Hey," he said as he sank down in the chair opposite Daniel's desk. "I had breakfast this morning at the café and saw two of our suspects in Dominique's attack case there."

"Which two?" Daniel asked.

"Burt Stanfield and Austin Colbert," Luke replied.

"I know Burt because he works in maintenance for the city, but I don't know Austin. Tell me your impression of him."

"Austin is about six feet tall and rather thin. I would say that physically he doesn't look like he would have the strength to carry a woman off somewhere, but I could be wrong."

"So, Burt is a much better candidate. I know he's burly and strong and could easily carry a petite woman like Dominique through the swamp," Daniel said.

"Right," Luke replied.

"I also don't know the other two men Dominique mentioned." Daniel flipped through the small notebook on his desk. "Jacob Benoit and Oliver LeBoeuf." He looked back at Luke. "Do you know either of them?"

"No, but I'd definitely like to get a look at them."

"Dominique said they were both fishermen. In fact, I was just about to get Clay and head to the swamp to interview them both. Want to tag along?" Daniel asked.

"Absolutely," Luke replied. He wanted…he needed to know who all the players were in Dominique's life. Of course, it was possible that none of the men she'd named was the guilty party. But he thought it was highly likely that one of them was the person who had tried what they now were sure was a kidnapping attempt on the woman he cared about.

It wasn't like he was in love with Dominique, but he considered her a close friend and he definitely cared what happened to her.

Fifteen minutes later, Luke was in the back seat of Daniel's car while Clay rode shotgun as they headed toward the swamp. As Daniel and Clay small-talked in the front seat, Luke stared out the window and thought about the men they were about to interview.

He was particularly interested in meeting Oliver LeBoeuf, a man Dominique had dated. Even though, according to her, their relationship hadn't lasted long, he still wanted to see the type of man Dominique had chosen to go out with.

Then he wondered why he was interested. It wasn't like he and Dominique were dating. As far as their lovemaking, it had been based solely on the very hot physical attraction that had simmered between them almost from the very beginning of their friendship. *Don't get weird about it*, he reminded himself.

So, they were friends with benefits, but he was determined there would be no more benefits between them in the future. The last thing they needed was to complicate their friendship. All he wanted now was to keep her safe, both from her nightly sojourns following Pierre and now from this new dangerous threat.

As Daniel parked in front of the swamp entrance, a rush of adrenaline flowed through Luke's veins. "Do you know where these men live?" he asked.

"No, I figured we'd stop by George's place. He seems to know where everyone lives in the swamp," Daniel replied.

George was George Trahan, a gator-hunter. It had been his new girlfriend who had tried to kill Angelique. Angelique and George had briefly dated. After they stopped, George had fallen in love with a woman named Desiree Augustine. Desiree had hated Angelique and was filled with a deadly rage. She believed George wouldn't truly be hers unless Angelique was dead.

With that thought in mind, one night she had gone to Angelique's shanty, the place where Dominique now lived, and had nearly succeeded in stabbing Angelique to death. Thankfully, Daniel had shown up and had gotten Desiree under arrest before that could happen.

The three lawmen now got out of the car and headed into the swamp. It was odd that so many people lived here, yet rarely did you see another person on the paths.

Hopefully, by now if the two men were morning fishermen, they'd be back in their shanties. If they were night fishermen, then they probably hadn't left their shanties yet.

It didn't take them long to reach George's shanty. Daniel knocked on the door and George answered. He stared at all three of them and then focused on Daniel.

"Am I in trouble?" he asked. Since Desiree's arrest, George had lost weight and looked rather haggard. He'd had no idea what Desiree had been up to, but he'd felt terrible that she'd attacked Angelique.

"No, nothing like that," Daniel said hurriedly. "We were hoping you could help us with some directions."

"Sure. What kind of directions do you need?" George asked, visibly relaxing.

"We want to find Jacob Benoit's shanty and Oliver LeBoeuf's place," Daniel replied.

"Yeah, I can help you with that," George said and then proceeded to give them directions to both the shanties. "Are they in trouble?"

"No, we just have a few questions to ask them to clarify something we're working on," Daniel replied. "Thanks for your help, George. See you later."

George went back inside. "We'll head to LeBoeuf's place first. It's on the way to Benoit's shanty." Daniel led the way as they got back on the main trail.

It didn't take them too long to find LeBoeuf's shanty. It was a relatively small, but neat place. The front of the shanty had been cleared from the encroaching swamp vegetation. Daniel knocked on the door and it was answered by Oliver. He had long dark hair that was tied back with a piece of rawhide.

Luke had to admit Oliver was a handsome guy with well-defined features and an athletic build. So, this was the man Dominique had dated. A wave of jealousy swept through Luke, surprising him.

Why on earth would he feel jealous? It wasn't like he and Dominique were dating or anything like that. They were just friends and he was working as her bodyguard when she went out at night. So, jealousy had no place at all in his head.

"What can I do for you all?" he asked, concern causing deep furrows to dance across his forehead.

Daniel introduced himself and Luke and Clay. "Mind if we come in? We have a few questions we'd like to ask you."

Oliver frowned. "Questions about what? Is this about Mystique's murder? I had absolutely nothing whatsoever to do with that."

"No, this isn't about Mystique. We have some questions for you about another matter," Daniel replied.

Oliver hesitated a moment and then allowed them to come inside. The interior of the shanty was neat and clean, although it smelled faintly of fish.

He gestured them to sit on the brown sofa and he took a seat in a chair across from them. "Now, what's this all about?"

"Dominique Santori," Daniel said.

One of Oliver's dark brows rose up. "Dominique? What about her?"

"We understand that you had a relationship with her about a year ago," Daniel said. Luke watched the man's face closely, looking for any tells that might expose something.

"Yeah, we dated for a little while," Oliver replied easily.

"We understand she broke it off with you. Were you upset when that happened?" Daniel asked.

"Well, yeah, I was upset. I was crazy about her, but that was a long time ago," Oliver replied. "You know, you can't make a woman love you if she doesn't, but I've moved on from her. Why? Did something happen to her?"

"She was attacked by somebody we believe intended to kidnap her," Daniel replied.

Oliver's eyes widened slightly. "But, she's okay?"

Daniel nodded. "She managed to fight the assailant off."

"Thank God," Oliver replied.

Daniel began to question him on his whereabouts at the time of the attack.

"I was here…in my home," Oliver replied.

"Were you with somebody or alone?"

"I was alone, but I swear I had nothing to do with the attack on Dominique. I would never do something like that to her," he said fervently.

For the next fifteen minutes, Daniel continued to drill the man with questions. Oliver's replies were all the same, indicating that he was either telling the truth or was a very good liar.

"I have one last question for you and then we'll leave you to the rest of your day. I see you have a bandage on your finger. What happened?" Daniel asked.

Luke hadn't even noticed the small bandage. He mentally kicked himself for not noticing it before now.

"Oh, yesterday I caught a fishhook in my finger," Oliver replied. "It was my own damn carelessness."

"Mind if I take a look at the wound?" Daniel asked.

Oliver took the bandage off and held out his finger. Both Daniel and Luke got up to take a closer look. Although small, it was a nasty wound. With Oliver's consent, Daniel took a picture of it and then the three left.

It was only when they were some distance away from the shanty that they stopped to discuss the interview. "What do you think?" Daniel asked Luke while Clay remained silent.

Luke frowned thoughtfully. "I believed he was innocent until I saw the wound. Dominique said she might have managed to stab the man assaulting her."

"So, was that a fishhook wound or a small stab wound?" Clay asked. His question hung in the air as they continued on their way to Jacob Benoit's shanty.

Was it possible that Oliver had never gotten over Dominique, that since their breakup he'd become obsessed with having her once again? Or was it possible the man was innocent and had really gotten a fishhook caught in his finger?

A deep frustration welled up in Luke. He hoped they would gain more clarity with the other men they interviewed. They had to catch the person before he acted again because the next time something like this happened, Dominique might not be as lucky.

Chapter Nine

For the next week and a half, each night Luke came to her shanty and they stalked Pierre through the marsh. However, to Dominique's frustration, Pierre still hadn't dug up the book she was so sure he'd stolen.

Luke had started coming to her place extra early so they had plenty of time to talk, time she enjoyed tremendously. Not only did she learn something new about him each time they had a deep conversation, they also laughed a lot, too. Twice during the week, they had gone to lunch together at the café.

She found him to be thoughtful and kind and funny. She also knew that when she was in his presence, she was absolutely safe from harm. When she wasn't in his presence, she continued to keep her guard up.

There were no more times when she allowed her mind to wander when she was out in the swamp by herself. She stayed focused on her surroundings, kept her knife clutched tight in her hand, and thankfully there had been no more kidnapping attempts.

Today was her day off and she was headed into town to do a little shopping at All That Jazz. Tonight, she was cooking dinner for Luke. She had to make a stop at the grocery store as well to get a couple of pork chops to make for him. And, she intended dinner to be served promptly at six.

She was lucky to find a parking space right in front of All That Jazz. She parked and then went inside the store.

"Hey, sis," Monique greeted her in surprise. At the moment they were the only two inside the place. "What are you doing here?"

"I could say I just stopped in to have a short visit with you, but the truth of the matter is I have a purse full of tip money and I'm in the mood to shop."

Monique grinned. "Well, then you've come to the right place. What are you looking for?"

"I don't know."

"That doesn't help me help you," Monique replied.

"How about I just browse for a few minutes," Dominique said.

"Browse away." Monique stepped back toward the register, and at that moment a couple of young girls came into the store.

While Dominique began flipping through the clothes on the sale rack, the girls went straight to the section of tops featuring tiny straps and cropped length. The style certainly wasn't for Dominique.

Monique helped them by telling them who would look good in what color. She had an eye for such things, which was why she was such a good salesperson.

Dominique moved from the sale rack to the loungewear, where she found a red two-piece outfit. The top was sleeveless and sleek and the pants were a bit wide and flowy. She loved it and it would be perfect for her to wear this evening before she changed into the boring dark clothes she wore to stalk Pierre.

She threw it over one arm and continued looking. By

the time she was finished, she had the red loungewear and a cute emerald-green blouse that matched Luke's eyes. The girls had left empty-handed amid much giggling.

"Good choices," Monique said as she rang up the items for Dominique.

"Thanks. Maybe some of your fashion flair is finally rubbing off on me," Dominique replied.

"Dom, you've always had good taste," Monique replied. Dominique paid and Monique placed the items into a sack. The two visited for a little while longer and then Dominique left to head to the grocery store.

It was another hot, humid day without a cloud in the sky. Thank goodness it was always cooler in the swamp. Dominique's shanty rarely got hot and there was often a slight breeze coming off the water.

It took her only minutes to arrive at Howard's Groceries. It was a relatively small place but it was the only food store in town and Howard stocked nearly everything a shopper would need.

She walked in and grabbed a basket and headed toward the meat section. As she looked at the pork selection, she couldn't help but notice Jacque LeBlanc standing nearby and looking over the steaks.

Jacque was something of a mystery. He was a tall, well-built, handsome man who lived deep in the swamp. He was a gator-hunter, but nobody knew much about him. Still, he supposedly knew a lot about what went on in the swamp.

Dominique made a mental note to herself. Maybe he was a man she should talk to concerning the attack on her. Maybe he knew something that would help them find the culprit.

Before she could approach him, he turned and wheeled

his basket in the opposite direction. Maybe it was better that she and Luke talked to the man together. She made another mental note to herself to mention it to Luke when she saw him later that evening.

She found a package of three nice-looking pork chops and put it in her cart, then headed to the canned vegetable aisle where she grabbed a can of carrots. She then went to the produce aisle where she got a sack of potatoes.

The last thing she bought was a large block of ice. Since there were no refrigerators in the swamp, most people used a big cooler with the ice as a refrigerator of sorts. The ice would last about a week and then she would have to buy another block.

She checked out and then got back in her car and headed home. She was actually looking forward to cooking for Luke tonight. From what he'd told her in one of their many conversations, most nights he simply zapped dinners in the microwave. Tonight, he would eat far better and that made her happy.

Happy. It was funny that she would feel happy. She was stalking a man she believed murdered her mother, she had some obsessed person stalking her and yet spending time with Luke had given her a happiness she hadn't felt for a long while.

It was going to be difficult to tell him goodbye when this was all over. She would miss their conversations and their laughter. Her evenings would become boring and lonely once again and she would be no closer to finding the man of her dreams, the one who would give her a happily-ever-after.

The physical chemistry between her and Luke still burned hot and bright but they hadn't made love again—

even though she would have liked to have him once again in her bed.

She pulled up and parked at the swamp's entrance. She'd have to juggle her bags or make two trips because she wanted one hand free to hold her knife as she walked home.

She got out of the car and pulled the bag with the ice over her left arm. She then grabbed the small shopping bag and her clothes bag and managed to get them over her left arm as well. Finally, she got her knife out of her purse and held it firmly in her right hand.

This was better than making two trips. She began the trek in, staying acutely aware of everything around her as she listened for any sounds of somebody approaching her.

Even though nothing had happened over the past week, she remained vigilant whenever she was outside by herself. She was determined she would not be a victim a second time.

As she reached the bottom of her bridge, she saw the piece of paper tapped to her door. Instantly, all her muscles tensed and her heart beat wildly as her gaze shot all around.

Seeing nobody lurking about, she hurried across the bridge and nearly screamed at the sight of a dead bird in front of her door. It looked as if its neck had been broken. The bird wouldn't have flown into her door and died accidentally. Its death looked deliberate. She grabbed the note from the door, stepped over the bird and went inside.

She immediately locked the door behind her, dropped all her packages on the floor and collapsed on the sofa, the note held in her trembling hand. The back of her throat closed up and she felt as if she couldn't draw a breath.

Who would be so cruel as to kill that poor bird? What

kind of a monster would wring the neck of an innocent creature? After several moments she finally felt steady enough to read what was written on the paper.

STOP SEEING THE LAWMAN. YOU BELONG TO ME.

The words seemed to jump off the page and once again her heart began to beat frantically as she dropped the note down on the coffee table.

She remained sitting on the sofa for several long minutes as she tried to get her fear under control. She didn't intend to call Luke. There was nothing he could do. Besides, he'd be here later and hopefully he could take care of the dead bird.

Stop seeing the lawman.

There was no way that was going to happen. Nobody and nothing was going to make her stop seeing Luke. She definitely didn't intend to obey some creep who had killed a poor bird and left her the note. Still, a new fear rushed through her. Did this mean Luke might be in danger?

Apparently, the person had been watching them to know she and Luke were spending a lot of time together. Dammit, who was doing this to her? Luke had told her Daniel had interviewed all the men who she'd named. None of them had a real solid alibi for the time of the last attack on her so any one of them could be guilty or all of them could be innocent.

She finally got up from the sofa and grabbed her groceries. She needed to get the ice and pork chops into the cooler. Once she'd taken care of that, she carried her clothing bag into her bedroom.

It was time for her to get her clothes changed and start cooking. She pulled on the new loungewear and then brushed her hair and put on a little mascara and then went out the back door to start her generator.

She stood for a few minutes on her deck, trying not to think about the note and the poor dead bird. Somehow in her mind, since over a week had passed with nothing happening, she'd hoped the person who'd tried to kidnap her had given up.

However, now she knew he hadn't given up. He'd been watching her movements, and apparently, he felt threatened by Luke's presence in her life.

She'd been afraid before. Now she was even more frightened. There was no question somebody was still after her, now making demands and watching her and waiting…waiting for the perfect opportunity to make her his own.

AS LUKE DROVE toward the swamp's entrance, he felt great. Tonight, he'd decided to wear a pair of black dress slacks with a green-and-black short-sleeved dress shirt. He had his surveillance clothes in a bag to change into later.

He'd decided to dress up a little because tonight was a special occasion—Dominique was cooking for him and she was even feeding him on his time, at six o'clock. Oh, she'd cooked bacon and eggs for him, but this just felt special and so he'd decided to dress up a bit.

The past week and a half had flown by. They'd gone out every night to follow Pierre. Unfortunately, he still hadn't dug up the missing client book.

Equally frustrating was the fact that Daniel and his men hadn't been able to pin down the man who had left the note and tried to kidnap Dominique. Still, he was grateful that no other attempts had been made on her and in that it had been a fairly peaceful ten days.

After today, his vacation time was over. He'd spoken with Daniel earlier in the day and they had decided he'd come in to work at nine-thirty in the mornings and work until four-thirty.

It was going to be difficult to work and still be there for Dominique during the nights, but he was really hoping he could talk her into stopping the nightly trips through the swamp. They'd been surveilling for over two weeks now without any success.

He reached the swamp's entrance and parked. He had stopped by the café earlier and had picked up a peach pie for dessert. In one of their many conversations she had mentioned she loved peach pie.

He grabbed the pie from the passenger seat and then picked up the bag containing his black jeans and black T-shirt. He then headed in, a rich anticipation rushing through him.

He was now quite familiar with the paths that would take him to her shanty. He walked quickly and it didn't take him long to reach her place.

He stopped short at the sight of a dead bird in front of her door. What the hell? Had the poor thing flown into the door and broke its neck? He knew occasionally birds might fly into a window, but a door?

A sense of dread filled him as he stepped over the bird and knocked on the door. "Dominique, it's me," he called out.

The lock disengaged and she opened the door. She looked positively stunning in a red outfit. The top hugged her breasts and showed off her slender build while the pants swirled around her long, shapely legs. Her hair was loose, but the smile she offered him appeared a bit forced.

"You look absolutely beautiful," he said.

"Thanks, you clean up nicely yourself," she replied. She opened the door wider to allow him entry and then closed and locked the door behind them.

"I come bearing a gift. It's a peach pie." He held it out to her.

"Thank you. This is very thoughtful of you." She took it from him and then led him to the kitchen, where she placed it in the center of the table.

"I couldn't help but notice the poor bird," he said as he sat in one of the chairs at the table.

"Yeah, I'm hoping maybe you could get rid of it for me, but we can talk about all that after dinner," she replied.

"Something sure smells good," he said. The air was redolent with the scent of cooking meat.

"That will be your dinner. We have smothered pork chops, crispy fried potatoes and honey-drizzled carrots. We also have corn bread with honey."

"Wow, that all sounds absolutely delicious," he replied. "Way better than a meal in a box that you zap in the microwave for five minutes."

She moved in front of a skillet on the electric burners. "It will be on the table at precisely six o'clock so you have about ten minutes to wait." She flashed a quick smile over her shoulder.

Despite the smile, he sensed a tension radiating from her, a tension he believed didn't have anything to do with her cooking dinner. Was it because of the dead bird? Or was he just imagining something that wasn't there?

The ten minutes passed fast as they small-talked about their days. She told him about shopping at All That Jazz and he talked about a book he'd been reading.

"If you'll hand me your plate, I'll fill it," she said.

He picked up the plate in front of him and gave it to

her. The table was already set with a platter of golden corn bread, butter and a bear-shaped bottle of honey.

She filled his plate with one of the chops, a healthy serving of the diced, crispy potatoes and the carrots. Once his plate was on the table, she filled her own and then sank down across from him.

"Dig in while it's hot," she said.

"It all looks delicious," he replied.

"Let's just hope it tastes delicious, too."

It took him only a couple of bites to assure her that everything was delectable. For a few minutes they ate in a comfortable silence. That was one of the things he liked about her—silence didn't intimidate or bother her.

When they were about halfway through the meal, they continued with their small talk. She offered him a second pork chop, but he was too stuffed to even consider it.

"I hope you saved room for a piece of your peach pie," she said when they finished eating.

"Maybe I'll have a piece a little later. Right now, I'm just too full," he replied. He still felt like something was slightly off with her this evening, but he figured if something was going on, she'd tell him in her own time.

Perhaps it was the dead bird. It had to have been shocking for her to discover it on her doorstep. Before he left here tonight, he would use a paper towel or something to move the bird from her door to someplace in the swamp.

"At least let me help with the cleanup," he said once they had finished eating.

"The best way you can help me is to stay out of my way. Just sit there and look pretty," she replied.

He laughed. "I'll sit here, but I don't know about the looking pretty part."

He watched as she efficiently cleared the table and

then washed the dishes using a large bottle of water and detergent. It always amazed him when he saw how the people who lived in the swamp had adapted to a life with little electricity and no running water.

"Have you ever thought about moving into town where you would have the convenience of a refrigerator and a dishwasher?" he asked.

"Sometimes it crosses my mind," she replied. She placed the last clean dish in the drainer and then they moved into the living room and sat on the sofa.

"I think more about it now, since Angelique has moved into town," she said, continuing the conversation. "She loves it, and I'm not sure if the appeal is because Daniel is there or that she can now take long, leisurely showers and use a dishwasher."

Luke laughed. "Maybe it's a combination of all of that. I will say it's nice to see Daniel so happy."

"Same with Angelique."

"I have a feeling Daniel is planning on proposing to her very soon, and I also have a feeling there will be a wedding before the end of the year," Luke said. "I'm curious," he continued. "When you get married, which sister will be your maid of honor?"

"Hopefully, by the time I get married Angelique is already married, then I'd have her stand with me as a matron of honor and Monique would be my maid of honor."

"Good decision," he replied. "Uh… I don't know if you realize it or not, but today is the last day of my vacation time."

She frowned. "Then you won't be available anymore to be my bodyguard during the nights."

"Daniel and I have worked my hours out so that I can still be here for you at night," he assured her. "Although I wish you'd stop the nightly stalking. Seriously, Dominique, tell me the truth. Aren't you growing tired of doing it?"

Her frown grew deeper, indicating a deep anguish. "But, my mother—"

"Wouldn't want you out doing this," he said, cutting her off.

She released a big sigh. "I'll admit I'm a bit tired of it, but if I don't do it, then how are you all going to prove Pierre is guilty?" Her doe-like eyes gazed at him intently.

God, he wished he had a good answer for her, but he didn't. "I don't know the answer to that right now," he admitted.

"I saw Jacque LeBlanc at the grocery store today, and I wondered if maybe it would be a good idea if we talked to him. Rumor has it he knows things about what goes on in the swamp. Maybe he knows something about the attacks on me."

"If he knows anything definitive, I believe he would have already come forward. Daniel and I spoke to him before about your mother's murder, but if you think it might be helpful, you and I could go to speak to him again about what's happening with you." He moved a little closer to her, wanting to be as supportive as possible.

She released a deep, heavy sigh. "Right now, I have more important things on my mind."

"Like what?" He reached out and took her hand in his. "Dominique, I've noticed you haven't quite been your sparkly self tonight."

Her fingers tightened around his for a long moment and then she pulled away and stood. "The dead bird wasn't the only thing left at my door this afternoon."

As she walked over to the bookcase, his heart thudded into the pit of his stomach. She grabbed a piece of paper just like the last note that had been left on her door and then rejoined him on the sofa and handed it to him.

STOP SEEING THE LAWMAN. YOU BELONG TO ME.

"Dammit, who is this bastard." He exploded with frustration.

"I don't know who he is, but he can't tell me what to do and I'm not about to stop seeing you whether we stop our nightly stalking or not." Her stubborn chin rose upward. "I'll see you as often as I want as long as you want to see me, too."

While that part of the note concerned him, far more concerning were the words *you belong to me*. It was a reminder that somebody out there wanted her and still posed a very real danger to her.

"Could this mean that you're in danger?" Once again, her gaze was intense as it held his.

"Don't you worry about me," he replied firmly. "I can take care of myself. I'll take the note with me when I leave and we'll check it for prints," he said.

"And you know there probably won't be any on it," she replied. "I'll go get a baggie." She got up and went into the kitchen and returned a moment later with the baggie in hand. He slipped the paper inside it and then set it back down.

"We'll check the alibis of all the men on our suspect list and see who has an alibi for this afternoon. Maybe that will help us shorten the list a bit."

She blew out another deep sigh. "I can't imagine what I've done to get the attention of this person. Have I been too flirtatious with the men in the café? I thought it was just all in good fun."

"Dominique, don't blame yourself for this, and I've

watched you and listened to you with your regular customers at the café and you don't do or say anything out of line with them," he replied firmly.

She once again reached out and took his hand in hers. "I swear, I don't know what I'd do without you right now, Luke."

He smiled. "I have a feeling you'd be just fine. You're not only a beautiful woman, Dominique, but you're also smart and incredibly strong."

A small laugh escaped her. "I'm not feeling so strong these days."

"You've been through a lot and here you are, still standing." He hoped she heard his admiration in his voice.

"I don't feel like standing right now. I think maybe I'll just stay in tonight and not torture you with a dark traipse through the marsh. In fact, even though it's relatively early, I think I'm ready to call it a day. Do you mind?"

"How can I mind? I got a great dinner and good conversation out of the evening." He stood and grabbed the note from the coffee table. "Are you sure you'll be all right?"

"I'll be fine. I'm on the breakfast shift in the morning so I'm just going to go to bed," she replied as she also got up from the sofa and walked with him to the front door.

He opened the door and then turned back to gaze at her. She looked tired. He raised a hand and cupped her cheek. She turned her head into the caress.

As the nights had passed, he'd tried not to touch her except for occasionally holding her hand as his desire to have her again still bubbled hot inside him, but he was determined not to make love with her again.

He finally removed his hand from her. "Since you're working the morning shift, I'll come in and eat breakfast. So, I'll just see you then," he said. He hated to leave her, but she hadn't asked him to stay and in any case, he shouldn't spend the night with her again. It would be far too big of a temptation to make another mistake. "Thanks for the delicious dinner."

"You're welcome. I wouldn't mind cooking for you again sometime soon, and now I'll just say good-night," she replied.

"Good night, Dominique." With that, he went out the door and nearly stepped on the dead bird. Dominique closed and locked the door behind him.

He'd grabbed a paper towel after dinner and he now pulled it from his pocket and bent down to pick up the dead bird. He gently scooped the poor thing up and carried it down the bridge.

He'd decided not to return the bird to the swamp. He would take it into the police station in the morning. It, along with the note, was evidence in Dominique's assault case. Pictures would be taken and then the bird would be disposed of.

When he reached his car, he placed the note and the bird on his passenger seat and then headed home. As he drove, his thoughts were scattered.

Stop seeing the lawman.

Was it possible the perp would come after him? Luke didn't think so. Whoever the man was, he was a damned coward, frightening a woman with notes and now the dead bird.

Was Dominique safe alone in her shanty? He knew the locks on her two doors were good and sturdy. They had both been changed after the attack on Angelique.

The windows would also be difficult to reach as most of them looked over the deck, which would be hard for anyone to access as the back door was the only way to get to the deck.

He believed she was as safe as she could be there, otherwise he would have been there for her full-time.

The events of the night played through him mind. She had looked so beautiful tonight in her red outfit. Still, he had hated the dark haunting that had been evident in the depths of her eyes.

He desperately wanted to fix things for her. He wanted Pierre under arrest for the murder of her mother. He needed to find the person who had attacked her with the intent to kidnap her. He wanted to fix her world so badly it ached inside his chest.

It was at that exact moment he realized he was deeply in love with Dominique Santori. He had no idea exactly when it had happened. He had believed he was keeping a healthy distance between them. But the truth of the matter was he had fallen hard for her.

His sudden awareness of his feelings for her shot a wave of warmth through him. The warmth only lasted a minute and then the reality of the situation washed a wave of cold despondency over him.

First of all, she hadn't indicated in any way that she was in love with him. Even if she was, it wouldn't matter. They weren't made for each other. He wasn't even sure he could live with her full-time.

He would be there for her if she wanted to continue with her nightly stalking of Pierre, and he would be there for her as she faced the threat of some creep who wanted her.

However, it was time he begin to emotionally distance himself from her. Already, he felt his heart breaking but the truth of the matter was he'd fallen in love with the wrong woman.

Chapter Ten

For the next three nights, Dominique stayed in and didn't go out to follow Pierre. That also meant she hadn't seen Luke for three nights. She had insisted he stay home and get some extra rest since he was now back on full duty with the police force.

The only place she was without her knife was when she was in the café working or when she was at home. She'd had several awkward conversations with her regulars, who had been questioned not only about the attack on her, but also about the day the note and dead bird had appeared at her door.

All of the men had claimed their innocence and they were appalled that she would even entertain the idea for one minute that they were guilty. Somebody was lying or the perp was somebody not even on her radar. And somehow, that was even more frightening.

Her days and nights were filled with a simmering fear, wondering when she might be attacked again. The only person she trusted completely was Luke, and tonight she was cooking for him once again.

She'd missed his company over the past three nights. She'd grown so accustomed to having him there to fill the hours of her evenings. She'd missed his laughter and the way he could make her laugh. She'd also missed their conversations about anything and everything.

She'd worked the morning shift and then stopped in the grocery store to pick up a few items. When she got back home, she was grateful there was no note on her door and nothing left on her doorstep. She'd packed her groceries away and then had taken a short—but nice—shower.

By the time she dressed in a pair of jeans and the new emerald green blouse she'd bought at All That Jazz, it was time to get into the kitchen and start preparing dinner.

On the menu tonight was fried fish, a broccoli rice, and a cucumber and tomato salad. She also intended to make skillet corn bread once again as Luke had loved it the last time she'd made it.

If she were honest with herself, she'd admit that she was hoping she could talk Luke into staying the night. As the days had passed, she'd yearned to be in his arms once again.

She wanted to feel his naked body against hers and make slow, sweet love with him. Then afterward she wanted to fall asleep in his arms as she knew that was the only place she truly felt safe and secure.

She knew Luke wanted her again, too. It was in his eyes when he gazed at her for any length of time. She felt it in his simplest of touches. The physical chemistry between them was still off-the-charts strong.

Eventually, it would all have to come to an end. If she decided to stop following Pierre, then there would be no more reason for Luke to come over each night. After the last three nights of not being out in the swamp, she was now reluctant to continue going out.

She'd come to the realization that catching Pierre digging up the missing book was a very long shot. As much as she wanted to see him behind bars for her mother's murder, she no longer believed she was the one who could get the evidence.

She wasn't a quitter, but she also wasn't ignorant. Besides, she was tired of spending hours of her nighttime, when she could be sleeping or reading a good book, watching a man who did nothing but fish and hunt gators.

In fact, tonight would be her goodbye to Luke. She knew he would continue to work on discovering who had tried to kidnap her, but he would no longer need to be her bodyguard at night.

He would probably be relieved. He would be able to go back to his regular hours and routine. The idea of no longer seeing him in the evenings broke her heart just a little bit, but releasing him from his bodyguard duties was the right thing to do.

She knew Luke wanted to find a special woman who would be his wife, but how could he find that woman with Dominique taking up all his nights? She realized now she'd been selfish. In her quest to catch her mother's killer, she hadn't thought about how much she had affected Luke's life.

She tried to push all her thoughts out of her head as she got busy preparing the evening meal. At ten to six, a knock fell on her door and she knew it was Luke.

He identified himself and then she unlocked and opened the door. As always, her heart fluttered a bit at the sight of him. He was clad in a pair of jeans and a dark green polo that emphasized his bright green eyes.

His slightly shaggy dark hair gleamed with rich highlights and she immediately wanted to dance her fingers through the silky strands. The scent of his delicious cologne radiated out from him and enveloped her with a sense of familiarity and comfort.

"I see you got the memo to wear green," she said as she led him to the kitchen.

"Great minds think alike," he replied with one of his gorgeous grins.

"Have a seat," she said. "Dinner will be ready in five minutes."

"Good thing I brought my appetite because everything smells really good." He sank into the chair he'd sat in the last time she'd made dinner for him. "So, how was your day?"

"Nothing exciting or troubling happened, so in that aspect it was a good day."

"That's what I like to hear," he replied.

"What about you?" She turned from the stovetop to look at him. "How was your day?"

"It was okay," he replied.

She turned back to the stove where everything was ready to serve. Instead of placing the plates on the table, she had them on the counter next to her.

The butter and honey and corn bread were already on the table, as was the cucumber and tomato salad. The fish was golden brown and she put several of the bigger pieces on his plate, along with a large serving of the broccoli rice.

"This all looks amazing," he said as she placed the plate in front of him.

She filled her own plate and then joined him at the table. "Eat up while it's warm," she said.

"You don't need to tell me twice," he replied and then used his fork to cut into a piece of the fish.

"Feel free to use your fingers. This is a manner-free zone."

He shot her another one of his dazzling grins, set down his fork and then picked up the fish by his fingers. Oh, she was going to miss that boyish grin of his.

The conversation was light and easy as they ate. He entertained her with more stories of when he had first become a police officer, making her laugh over and over again.

They finished the meal and she cleaned up the mess, then they moved into the living room where they both sat on the sofa. "So, are we going out into the swamp tonight?" he asked.

"No, and I'm ready to give up on spying on Pierre," she replied.

He sat up straighter and looked at her in surprise. "What made you decide to stop?"

"I just realized how futile it is. Like you told me before we even started following him. I could watch him for months and he might never dig up the book." She shifted her position, bringing her a bit closer to him. "I don't want to waste any more of my time, but I especially don't want to waste any more of yours. I've been quite selfish in using you as my bodyguard."

"There isn't a selfish bone in your body," he replied in protest. "You were just hurting and frustrated, but never selfish."

"I'm still hurting and frustrated, but I'm also tired of traipsing through the swamp on the off chance we'll get lucky."

He took her hand in his, his eyes glittering like bright emeralds. "I promise you we will get justice for your mother and that we'll find the creep who is after you."

She squeezed his hand and smiled. "You're a very nice man, Luke Madison."

"I try to be," he replied and then released her hand. He studied her for a long moment. "I guess this means I won't be seeing as much of you."

"You can now spend your evenings looking for that special woman you want in your life," she replied, surprised by a small pang of sadness that resonated inside her. She told herself it was just because he'd been such a big part of her world. Habit. He was a habit that it was time she break.

"Just because we aren't going into the swamp at night doesn't mean I can't occasionally invite you to lunch or dinner at the café," he replied.

"And I suppose I wouldn't mind occasionally cooking dinner for you," she added. There was no reason why she had to go completely cold turkey and never spend any time with him again.

He smiled at her. It was a soft smile that sparkled in the gold shards of his eyes and shot an unexpected warmth into her heart. "Then we'll still see each other," he said.

"Since this is kind of our last official night together, do you want to spend the night?" she asked. She stared at him intently, wanting this one last night with him.

He sat back on the sofa, a pained expression on his features. "Dominique, we both know that's not a good idea."

"It would just be a final, casual hookup," she replied, hoping to entice him into staying. "It doesn't have to mean anything."

"It's still not a good idea," he replied.

Disappointment rushed through her. She had so hoped to have one last time in his arms, but obviously he wasn't keen about it and she certainly wasn't going to beg.

"So, what does your work schedule look like for the rest of the week?" he asked.

They small-talked for another half an hour or so, but things suddenly felt awkward between them. She felt as if they were two strangers making nice with each other instead of friends who had spent an inordinate amount of time together. It was almost a relief when he indicated it was time for him to leave.

She walked with him to the door, disappointment mingling with sadness inside her. "Luke, thank you. I've truly appreciated everything you've done for me," she said.

"No need to thank me. I've enjoyed my time with you," he replied. "If you ever think about going back out there to follow Pierre, I want you to call me and I'll come to be your bodyguard."

She forced a smile and then released a small laugh. "Why do I feel like I'll never see you again when we live in a little town and I'll probably see you tomorrow."

He grinned at her. It was that charming smile that she'd always loved. "You're right, you'll probably see me tomorrow. Now that I know you're working the mid-shift, I intend to eat my lunch in your section. I'll complain about the food and the service and I'll leave you a five percent tip," he said, repeating his fake threats.

She couldn't help but laugh. "You are such a goofball."

He reached up as if to cup her cheek, but dropped his hand back to his side and instead opened the door. "Good night, Dominique," he said as he turned back to her. "You know I'm here for you. As I've told you before, if something happens that frightens or concerns you, then call me."

"I will. Good night, Luke."

He disappeared out the door and she closed and locked

it behind him. She went back to the sofa and collapsed into the corner.

The fact that he'd turned down the offer to stay the night with her, to be intimate again with her made her realize that it was possible she really had only been a job to him.

Sure, they'd been intimate the one time, but maybe he'd only slept with her because he was curious and wanted to explore his physical desire for her. He'd satisfied his curiosity and now he was done with that aspect of their relationship.

A wave of unexpected sadness swept through her. She hadn't expected it would be so difficult to tell him goodbye. But now it was done and it was time she think about her future.

Maybe it was time she started dating. Maybe it was time for her to agree to go out with some of the men who had invited her out over the past few months. One of them could be the man of her dreams…the one who would give her children and a happily-ever-after.

If she was ever going to find a husband, the only way she could do it was to begin dating again. Would Luke start dating now that his evenings belonged to himself again?

She knew he wanted to find that special woman, the one who would fit into his life of routine and structure. She could only wish him well because more than anything she wanted to see Luke happy.

Gutted, Luke sat in his car, not yet ready to drive home. He stared at the swamp entrance, now barely discernable with the darkness of night falling.

While he had wanted her to agree to stop going out in

the swamp chasing after Pierre, he was now faced with the realization that he would no longer be spending his evenings with her. Even though he knew it was for the best, that didn't stop the heartache that rode with him as he finally started his car and began the drive home.

When she'd asked him to stay the night, he'd been so tempted to agree. He would have loved to hold her in his arms once again, to taste the sweet heat of her lips and to make love with her one last time.

It had been his overwhelming love for her that had stopped him. He'd recognized that he didn't want another memory of her to keep him mourning her and his ill-fated love. It had been that, plus the fact that she'd said it would just be casual. He couldn't do casual anymore with her.

He'd been a fool to let her get so far into his heart. He should have protected himself more. She'd never indicated to him that their relationship was anything other than casual for her.

It was time now that he move on with his life and somehow, someway get over loving Dominique. He had a feeling that was going to be a difficult thing to do.

By the time he got home, he was exhausted. It was a mental tiredness coupled with the heavy weight of his heart. He would miss their conversations and their shared laughter. He would miss the very scent of her and the way her facial features displayed her every emotion.

That night, it took him a very long time to fall asleep, and when he did sleep, he fell into dreams of dancing in the rain with her.

He awakened early and for the first time in a long time he was at the police station early. It was just after seven when he walked into the murder room where Clay and Daniel were already seated.

Both men looked at him in surprise. "Hey, Luke. You're here early this morning," Daniel said.

"Yeah, Dominique didn't go out in the swamp last night so I got home at a decent time." He sank down in the chair between the two men. "In fact, she's decided she's done stalking Pierre."

"Really? Well, that's really good news," Daniel replied. "If it's true. Are you sure she's really done?"

"Yeah, I'm sure," Luke said.

"Well, that's one less thing for us to worry about and I get back one of my best officers. A win-win situation as far as I'm concerned." Daniel took a sip from his coffee cup.

"We've got plenty of other things to worry about," Clay said. "Like finding the creep who's after her and getting some evidence so we can make an arrest in Mystique's murder."

"I still don't know how we're going to get any evidence to prove Pierre's guilt beyond a reasonable doubt." Daniel frowned.

"Somehow, someway, something is going to break in the case," Clay said optimistically. "Maybe Pierre will get drunk one night with his fishing buddies and he'll let something slip."

"We can only hope something like that happens," Daniel replied.

"Right now, I'm more concerned about Dominique's safety." Even saying her name aloud ached in Luke's heart.

"Too bad we haven't been able to pin down solid alibis with all the potential suspects she gave us," Daniel said, his frown cutting across his forehead. "It would be nice if we could at least rule out some of those men."

"What I worry about is that none of them are guilty and the perp is somebody not even on our radar," Luke replied.

"We just have to keep working the case and see what pops up," Daniel said.

"I don't want to wish anything bad on Dominique, but it would almost be helpful if the perp left another note or something for her," Clay said. "Maybe the next time he'll get sloppy and leave me some nice prints."

"As long as it's just a note or something like that. Of course, my biggest concern is that there will be another kidnapping attempt and this time he'll be successful." The very idea of that tightened all of Luke's stomach muscles and made him half sick. "So, what's on today's agenda?"

Daniel released a deep sigh. "We do our usual patrol. Keep your eyes and ears open for any information that might help in either of the cases. Then, why don't we plan to meet back here right before lunch time."

All three of them stood. While Daniel headed down the hallway toward his office, Luke and Clay headed out the back door.

"It's going to be nice to have you back here where you belong," Clay said.

"Thanks. I have to admit, I'm glad to be back in my regular routine," Luke replied. Routines he clung to… routines that assured he would never be the right man for Dominique.

In the mornings, Luke was usually on foot patrol. He headed down a very quiet Main Street. It was too early for the stores to be open and so the sidewalks were void of people.

The only place where there was any activity at all was

the café, where already cars were parked as people went in to enjoy an early breakfast.

Dominique wouldn't be there yet. He knew from talking to her last night that she was working the mid-shift. Was his plan to eat lunch at the café today because he was hungry for the food? Or was he just hungry to see her again?

By nine o'clock, Main Street began to fill up as shoppers arrived and stores opened. Luke greeted the people he met as he walked. He stopped and went into the feedstore, where he visited for a few minutes with the owner, Ben Jackson.

He always tried to stop in some of the stores and speak with the owners or whoever was working. It was part of Daniel's plan to keep relations good between the police department and the business owners.

As he stepped out of the store, he ran into Nola Fontenot. "Good morning, Officer Madison," she greeted him cheerfully.

"Morning, Nola. How are you doing on this fine day?"

"Oh, I'm doing okay. Of course, I'm just waiting for you all to do your job and get that murderer Pierre Guidry under arrest."

"We're doing the best we can," Luke replied.

She cast him a sly smile. "I understand you've been spending a lot of time with Dominique."

Luke's heart squeezed tight. "Yeah, I was helping her out with an issue, but now that issue is resolved and so I won't be seeing that much of her."

"Oh, that's too bad, I know how much she was enjoying spending time with you," Nola replied. "You know, I've known the Santori women since they were babies.

They are a fine bunch and now that Mystique is gone, I think of those girls as my very own."

"I know how close you were—are—to all of them," Luke said.

"Well, I'd better be on my way. I have a few errands to run and I always like to be back in my shanty during the heat of the day."

"I'll see you later, Nola." He watched as the plump woman headed on down the sidewalk. He was glad she'd moved on, for talking to her only reminded him of Dominique.

The morning passed uneventfully and at eleven thirty, he returned to the police station. It was difficult for him to think that tonight he wouldn't cross Dominique's bridge with the sweet anticipation of seeing her again.

He met Daniel and Clay in the break room. "How about we all head to the café for lunch?" Daniel suggested, as if reading Luke's mind.

"Sounds good to me," Clay said agreeably.

"Me too."

"So, did either of you encounter any trouble on your morning patrols?" Daniel asked once they were in his car and headed down the street to the café.

"I spoke to Nola, who once again berated us for not doing our job and getting Pierre under arrest," Luke said.

"And I wrote out a speeding ticket to Alex Whitmeyer. I clocked him going seventy miles an hour on Magnolia Drive, where the speed limit is fifty-five," Clay said. "The little snot told me his parents would speak to the prosecuting attorney and he wouldn't have to pay the fine and wouldn't be in any trouble."

Daniel snorted. "That kid thinks just because his parents have money, no rules apply to him."

"That's all I've got to report," Clay said.

"That's it for me, too," Luke added.

By that time, they'd reached the café. Luke saw her the moment they walked in. As always, she looked stunning in the pink T-shirt and jeans that was her uniform when at work. She was waiting on an older couple Luke didn't know.

Daniel chose a booth in her section and they all settled in. Luke didn't know why anxiety filled him at the prospect of just ordering his lunch from her. After all, he had just seen her the night before.

Then she was there, smiling at them all and his heart expanded with his love for her. "Hi, Luke," she said, her beautiful chocolate eyes lingering on him for a long moment.

"Hey, Dominique," he replied.

She took their orders and then left their booth. She returned with their drinks and then a few minutes later with their food.

As they ate, the discussion was about things going on in town. A fall festival was planned in another month. It was a day when the streets filled with people. Not only did the stores run sidewalk sales, but local artists and craftsmen would sell their wares as well.

While they talked and ate, Luke couldn't help but look at Dominique again and again. In spite of his personal feelings for her, she was a joy to watch as she smiled or laughed with the customers she served.

Was the person who had written her the notes and tried to kidnap her in the café right now? Luke's stomach muscles tightened as he did a slow glance around the room. There was only one of the regulars she'd named there.

Jacob Benoit sat alone at a two-top. The fisherman had

been interviewed concerning his whereabouts on the dates in question. His alibi had been like the others. He'd been in his shanty alone at the times of the attack and when the notes had been left.

They finished eating and then headed back to the station. On the short drive back, Luke decided that was the last meal he'd eat in the café for a while. It was just too painful to see her and know she didn't love him.

He realized he wanted—he—needed to keep busy. He desperately needed his mind focused on other things. Whenever there was a quiet moment, his head filled with thoughts of Dominique, and the heartbreak would come crashing down on his head all over again.

They had just gotten back and settled in the murder room when Gus called from the front desk. "I got a man here who wants to talk to the person in charge of the Santori murder."

The three men looked at each other. Was it possible that finally this was the break they'd been waiting for? Could the man tie Pierre to the murder scene? Had Pierre finally made a mistake and talked to somebody about the murder?

"Send him to my office," Daniel said as he stood. He hung up the phone. "You two come with me. Let's hear what this man has to tell us."

The three of them hurried up the hall to Daniel's office, where Daniel sat behind his desk. Luke and Clay stood against the wall, leaving the chair in front of the desk for the new visitor.

They all had just settled in place when a knock fell on the door. Clay opened it and a tall man Luke had never seen before entered.

Daniel stood and held out his hand. "I'm Chief of Police, Daniel LeCroix, and these are two of my officers, Luke Madison and Clay Caldwell."

The man grabbed hold of Daniel's hand and shook it. "Lucien Rousseau is my name and I'm a fisherman by trade."

"Please, have a seat, Mr. Rousseau." Daniel gestured to the chair before him.

Lucien Rousseau looked to be in his mid-forties. His long dark hair was tied back at the nape of his neck and his features were bold and well weathered. He was also missing one of his front teeth.

"I understand you might have some information that would help in solving the murder of Mystique Santori."

"I do."

"Is this something you heard or learned recently?"

"No, I've known about it for months," Lucien replied.

"Might I ask what took you so long to come in?" Daniel asked.

"A couple months ago I got a gig on an offshore fishing boat. The work was hard but the pay was good. I just got back to my shanty yesterday and got caught up with all the swamp gossip."

They spoke for a couple of minutes about the name of the offshore boat and exactly who had employed Lucien. Daniel asked him several questions concerning his employment.

"Enough about me." Lucien suddenly leaned forward in the chair. "I heard you're wanting to put Pierre Guidry away for killing Mystique."

"We definitely believe he's guilty of her murder," Daniel said.

"Well, you're wrong. You're all wrong. He didn't kill Mystique. He's not guilty," Lucien finished flatly. Luke felt as if the bottom of his stomach fell out at the man's words.

"H-how do you know he isn't guilty?" Daniel asked, obviously stunned by the man's words.

"Because on the night and time she was murdered, I saw him fishing in the honey hole he thinks is a big secret. He keeps a pirogue there hidden under some brush. Sometimes, when he goes out in the pirogue to hunt the big gator he wants to catch, I fish off the bank there."

"Are you sure you saw him on the right night?" Daniel asked.

"Positive, because when I woke the next morning, I heard the Voodoo Queen was dead and then I left to get on the fishing boat." Lucien flashed his dark eyes to each one of them. "I got no friendship with Guidry and no reason to come in here except I don't want to see an innocent man go to jail for a murder he didn't commit. Pierre isn't your man and that's all I got to say."

Abruptly he stood. "And now it's time for me to go. I got a wife who is mad I stayed out and away from home for so long and kids clamoring to spend some time with me. If you got more questions for me, you can find me at my shanty in the swamp."

On that note, he opened the door and stepped out and then closed the door behind him. For a long moment, a stunned silence reigned among the three of them.

"Did you believe him?" Luke finally broke the silence.

"I'm not sure," Daniel replied slowly.

"If he's right, then we're no closer to solving the murder than we were on the night it happened," Clay said dismally.

"Before we jump to any conclusions, we need to thoroughly check out Lucien's story," Daniel said. "Clay, why don't you look into the offshore fishing boat. See if you can find out when he was hired and when he left the boat."

"Got it," Clay said.

"And Luke, why don't you head into the swamp and see what you can find out about the relationship between Guidry and Lucien," Daniel continued. "Talk to George and any other men you come across. If it turns out that Lucien and Pierre are close, then I'll be less likely to believe this new alibi for Pierre."

"And if they aren't close?" Luke's question hung in the air.

Daniel released a deep sigh. "Then we'll have to face the fact that we might have been chasing the wrong man for the murder."

Luke felt as if the entire world was exploding apart. The murder they believed they had solved was no longer a sure thing, and he'd fallen deeply in love with a woman he knew he couldn't live with and who didn't love him back.

HE WAS READY. He was so ready to make her his own. Even though he had only communicated with her so far with the notes he'd left for her, she obviously cared about him, too. She'd stopped seeing the lawman, just like he'd told her to do. That proved to him that she wanted to please him.

Every time he saw her, she half stole his breath with her beauty. She was cheerful and lively and that's what he needed, that's what his house needed.

Once she was here where she belonged, there would be no more loneliness for him, no more grief to deal with. Her bright energy would fill up all the dark places in his house, and more importantly, all the dark places in his heart.

He needed her and he was ready to take her again.

Only this time it wouldn't matter if she had a knife. Once he pierced her skin with the injection he had ready, there would be no fight. She would fall into his arms and he would bring her here, to be his forever more.

Now it was just a matter of waiting for the right time and place. He would find that right time very, very soon. And he couldn't wait. A sweet anticipation rushed through his body.

Soon, she would finally be his and his alone, and with enough time he would make her love him. Oh yes, all his dreams were about to come true. The beautiful Dominique would be his. She would fulfill the promises that had been broken by another. She would be his through eternity.

Chapter Eleven

Dominique sat with her two sisters on the sofa in her shanty, waiting for Daniel to arrive with an update on their mother's case.

It was the first time he'd called them all together and all three of them were hopeful that Daniel was bringing them good news. Of course, the best news of all would be that they had found the evidence they needed to get Pierre behind bars.

She was hungry for something good to happen. Since Luke had walked out of her house two nights before, she had been filled with a sadness she didn't understand and couldn't quite shake.

She missed Luke desperately. He'd taken a big piece of her heart with him and had left behind an aching emptiness she certainly hadn't expected.

Angelique now looked at Dominique. "You've certainly been quiet this evening."

"Yeah, you haven't been your normal bubbly self tonight," Monique added.

"I'm just tired. I didn't sleep well last night and then I worked the early shift this morning," Dominique replied.

"You haven't mentioned your nightly stalking of Pierre lately," Angelique observed.

"That's because I gave it up a few nights ago," she replied.

"Thank the lord," Monique replied and placed a soft hand on Dominique's. "I was so worried about you when you were doing that at night. Even taking Luke with you didn't make me feel much better about it."

"I felt completely safe with Luke by my side," she said. Again, a pang of sadness shot off in her. What was wrong with her? Why couldn't she straighten out her emotions? "Didn't Daniel give you an idea about why he wanted to meet with us?" she asked Angelique.

"No, he didn't. He just called me at the store and told me to meet him here," she replied. There it was...that love she had for her boyfriend so rich in her tone.

Dominique wanted that for herself, but she didn't feel like dating at the moment. Still, how was she ever going to find her person if she spent all her evenings alone in her shanty?

A knock fell on the door and Dominique hurried to answer it. Not only was it Daniel, but Luke and Clay were with him, as well.

Luke looked wonderfully handsome in his blue uniform, but she refused to let her gaze linger on him. She missed him so much. Her life just wasn't the same without him in it.

"Gentlemen, have a seat," she said. She gestured to the chair across from the sofa and then hurried into the kitchen to grab two more chairs.

Clay met her halfway and took the chairs from her and carried them into the living room. "My love, what's up?" Angelique asked once everyone was seated.

"We've had a new development in your mother's murder case," Daniel said.

"A new development?" Dominique leaned forward, eager to hear the news. She kept her gaze fixed on Daniel. Maybe this was what they'd all been waiting for. Maybe they'd finally arrested Pierre.

Daniel frowned. "Unfortunately, somebody has come forward to alibi Pierre for the night and time of the murder."

Dominique stared at him, as if he'd suddenly begun speaking a foreign language. She leaned back against the sofa, stunned by this unexpected news.

"What are you talking about?" Angelique asked.

"Who's come forward and why now after all this time?" Monique asked.

Dominique looked at Luke as the floor beneath her feet fell out from under her. How she wished she could be in his arms right now as the world tilted and half dizzied her.

"The man's name is Lucien Rousseau," Daniel said. "Do any of you know him?"

They all shook their heads and listened as Daniel told him about the man working on an offshore fishing boats since the day after the murder until yesterday when he'd come in to speak to them.

"I looked into his story about spending time on the offshore boat. I spoke to the captain of the boat, who confirmed Lucien's story," Clay said.

"And I checked out the relationship between Lucien and Pierre and from everything I heard, the two men didn't have much of a personal relationship," Luke added.

"Therefore, we have no reason not to believe Lucien's story that he saw Pierre out at his fishing hole on the date and time of your mother's murder," Daniel said.

"So that means you all are back to square one," Dominique said in deep frustration. How many hours of her life had been wasted foolishly shadowing an innocent man? Still, she couldn't regret that time, for it had given her Luke for a little while.

"Are there any new suspects in the case?" Monique asked.

"None, but we're going to get there. I swear to God I'll find the person responsible for Mystique's murder," Daniel said fervently.

Dominique knew he meant well, but now there was no real suspect in the case and justice for her mother might never come. Again, her grief welled up inside her.

What she wanted now was to collapse in Luke's strong arms. She wanted him to caress his hands up and down her back in an effort to soothe the disappointment inside her. But she couldn't ask him to do that, and in any case, it wasn't long after that the three men left, taking Angelique with them so she could go on home with Daniel.

"I guess we'll all just be in limbo longer," Monique said. She gave Dominique a quick hug. "I know how disappointed you must be. I know you truly believed Pierre was the killer."

"I am terribly disappointed. I was so certain he was guilty and I know you're disappointed as well," Dominique replied.

"I am, but they still have another suspect…remember there's Charles Lathrop," Monique said.

"I just don't believe Charles killed her in such a horrid way because he thought the love spell she cast for him didn't work." Dominique released a deep sigh.

"On another note, things seemed to feel a little tense and strange between you and Luke tonight. What's going on with that?" Monique studied her.

"Nothing's going on. Since I decided not to follow

Pierre anymore, there's really no reason for us to keep seeing each other."

Monique's gaze continued to hold Dominique's. "And you're good with that?"

"Of course. It's time he get back to his life and I get back to mine," she replied, even as she felt the hot burn of tears behind her eyes. What on earth was wrong with her? "I'm just sorry I wasted his time foolishly chasing after Pierre."

"You were doing what you believed was right," Monique replied. Monique stood. "Guess I'll just head on home."

Dominique got up and walked her sister to the door. "Are you going to be okay walking home?"

Monique released a small laugh. "I'll be just fine. I'm not afraid of the dark and I'm far stronger than you and Angelique give me credit for. Besides, I don't have a creep bothering me like you do. You stay safe and we'll talk tomorrow."

She opened the door and the two sisters said their goodbyes, then Monique disappeared into the darkness outside. Dominique closed and locked the door behind her.

She sank back down on the sofa and found herself once again fighting back tears. Why was she so emotional? It wasn't like she was pregnant. She didn't think she was having a mental breakdown, so what was bringing tears to her eyes so often?

Maybe it was just because there was so much going on in her life right now. She had just learned that the man she'd believed had killed her mother was probably innocent. She had a dangerous man trying to kidnap her and make her his own, and she still grieved for the mother she had lost. It was enough to make a grown woman emotional.

Even though she was working the dinner shift the next day and it was still early in the evening, she decided to go to bed. Only in sleep did she escape the tears that haunted her far too often lately.

She awoke early the next morning and turned on her generator so she could get some coffee brewing. Once the coffee was ready, she poured herself a cup and then sat on the deck to watch the sunrise.

It was always quite stunning at this time in the morning as the sun rose just enough to send golden rays across the landscape. The dark water beneath her lit up as if it had swallowed a lantern. Fish jumped, telling her good morning with their splashes.

Morning birds sang from the top of the tupelos and bald cypress trees. The waves lapped against the wooden stilts that held the shanty up, creating a pleasant, rhythmic sound that was as soothing as the squeak of a rocking chair.

She sipped her coffee, her mind filled with the beauty of the swamp and nothing more. The Spanish moss that draped from the trees sparkled in the soft glow from the sun.

This was what would be hard to leave behind if she ever decided to move into town. Granted, it would be far more convenient for her coming and going to work if she got an apartment in town. But it would be hard to leave the place that had cradled her since her birth.

She finished her coffee and then moved inside and got out the two-top cooking burners to make her breakfast. She had nothing on her agenda today until she had to go into work at two.

After she ate a breakfast of scrambled eggs and toast, she cleaned up the kitchen and then took a shower. She dressed in one of her housedresses and then sank down on the sofa with a book she wanted to read.

She needed to keep her mind occupied and reading was the perfect way to do that. It wasn't long before she was captivated by the story unfolding in the book.

Time slipped by and before she knew it, it was time to get ready to go to work. As she dressed in her jeans and the official Dark Waters Café pink T-shirt, she congratulated herself on getting through the day without thoughts of Luke.

Surely it was just going to take some time, and then she'd eventually stop missing his presence in her life.

It had been a while since she'd worked an evening shift. When she'd been chasing after Pierre, she had requested to work only mornings and afternoons, but now she was back to her normal routine and that often had her working in the evenings.

She got to work and for the next six hours she put on a happy face and served her customers with care. None of her regulars were there, which made her time more pleasant.

There was still an awkwardness between her and the men she used to banter and tease with. She felt a wariness when she served them now, as she wondered who was tormenting her with scary notes and dead birds. Who had thrown a burlap bag over her head with the intention of kidnapping her?

By the time her shift ended, she was exhausted. The café seemed to have been particularly busy tonight. She stepped out of the back door to head to her car that was parked next to the large trash container in the corner of the lot.

It was just a little after eight when she got home. She changed out of her work clothes and into one of the housedresses she favored when she was home alone.

Even though she was tired, she wasn't ready for bed yet. She picked up the book she'd been reading and curled up in the corner of the sofa.

She'd only been reading a few minutes when a knock sounded at her door. She frowned and her heart beat a little quicker as she stood. Who would be at her door at this time of night? Friend or foe?

She walked to the door. "Who is it?"

"Dominique, it's me… Luke."

Relief fluttered through her and she quickly unlocked the door and opened it. "Luke, what are you doing here?" she asked. He was clad in a pair of jeans and a red T-shirt and as he entered the shanty, he filled it with his familiar scent.

She closed the door after him. "I just wanted to check in with you," he replied.

She gestured toward the sofa. "Do you want something to drink?"

"No thanks, I'm good." He sank down on the sofa and she joined him there. "I wanted to see how you were doing since Pierre was alibied for your mother's murder?" His soft gaze held hers for a long moment.

She broke the connection and looked at a space just over his head. "At first, I was so shocked. You know how much I believed he was guilty." She looked back at him. "Now I'm just depressed that we have no idea who killed her."

"I just wanted to let you know that we're starting all

over again and tearing our investigation apart to see if there's something we missed. We'll find the guilty party, I swear we will," he said fervently. "Your mother needs justice."

She smiled. "I hope eventually you'll get it for her. I had just hoped it would be sooner rather than later."

"I know, and I'm so sorry," he replied.

She leaned back from him. "So, have you started your hunt for that special woman you want in your life?" she asked lightly.

His gaze grew especially intense on her. He was silent for a long moment before finally speaking. "I don't need to hunt for her. I already found that special woman. I am in love with you, Dominique."

His words positively stunned her. She hadn't seen it coming. "Surely you're mistaking lust for love," she replied.

"That's not true. I know the difference between physical desire and love, and I am deeply, madly in love with you," he replied and leaned toward her, enveloping her in his achingly familiar scent.

"Oh Luke, it would never work between us," she said softly. Despite the warmth that had filled her heart at his words of love, she was a realist.

"I am not the special woman for you and you aren't the special man for me. I need a mate who is spontaneous and unstructured. And you need a woman who can live in the world of routines and structure. We'd be divorced before the writing on the marriage certificate dried."

He stared at her for a long moment and then slowly nodded his head. "Of course, you're right," he said, the brilliance of his eyes dimming a bit. He stood, obviously uncomfortable now that he'd spoken of his love for her. "Well, I guess I'll head on home."

She got up from the sofa and followed him to the front door. Her heart was unusually heavy. She couldn't be in love with him. Could she? Even if she was, it wouldn't change their situation.

He reached the door first, unlocked it and then opened it. He turned back to face her and his eyes still held a sadness that broke her heart.

"I'll be in touch concerning the two cases," he said.

"Thank you, I appreciate it."

"Dominique, if you get scared or something happens you aren't sure of, please don't hesitate to call me. Above all, I want you to be safe."

"I'll call if I need to," she replied.

"Good night, Dominique."

"Good night, Luke."

With that, he walked out of the door and into the darkness of the night.

She closed and locked the door behind him, her emotions a jumbled mess. She'd never meant for him to fall in love with her. Many times, they had talked about how different they were and how they had different needs in the person they would marry. She'd tried to keep things casual with him. Dammit, he wasn't supposed to fall in love with her.

She sank down on the sofa once again. She refused to consider her own emotions where he was concerned. It didn't matter how she felt about him. She knew they were not a match. She just didn't understand why she suddenly felt like crying.

Gutted. Luke was once again absolutely gutted as he left her shanty and headed back to his car. He hadn't meant to speak of his love for her, but he'd been unable to hold it inside him any longer.

She'd looked so pretty in the pink-and-yellow flowered house dress, with her hair loose around her shoulders and down her back.

But it wasn't her physical beauty that had made him fall in love with her. It was her kindness and the way she cherished her family. He'd fallen in love with her sense of humor and her intelligence. There were so many things that had drawn him to her.

And now, more important than ever, he had to figure out how to stop loving her. In his heart of hearts, he knew she was right about them. They would never work. But that hadn't stopped him from falling deeply in love with her.

She would be a deep ache in his heart for a very long time to come. Besides, she hadn't told him she was in love with him. It was obvious that she wasn't by how easily she had dismissed the idea of a romance between them.

He finally got home and went directly to bed, hoping she wouldn't visit his dreams. He awoke early the next morning, eager to get into the station.

The least he could do for the woman he loved was find the person who had killed her mother. He needed to immerse himself in not only that case, but in the case that was even more important. He needed to figure out who wanted her so badly he'd attempted to kidnap her.

By seven he was back in the murder room with Daniel and Clay. A pall of disappointment draped over them like a heavy shroud. It had been like this since the moment Lucien Rousseau had come forward with his alibi for Pierre.

The setback in the case had made them all sick. They

had been so sure that Pierre was their man, that he had been the one who'd murdered Mystique, but now they were back to square one.

"So, what's the general thought now about Charles Lathrop?" Daniel asked.

"I never really thought he was a good contender in the first place," Luke admitted. "He's definitely an arrogant creep, but I didn't believe he'd kill Mystique just because the love spell she cast for him didn't work."

"Maybe he figured out that his personality made the love spell not work," Clay added drily, causing both Daniel and Luke to laugh.

"Then where do we go from here?" Clay asked.

"Like I said yesterday, we start the investigation all over again. Hopefully we can look at things with fresh eyes. We all decided on Pierre's guilt early on and now that he's off our suspect list, we need to look hard at everyone else who was in Mystique's life at the time of the murder," Daniel said.

"And I don't believe some stranger wandered in and killed her," Clay said. "Her throat was sliced and that's a very personal way to kill someone. Somebody was filled with a tremendous rage when they killed Mystique Santori."

"Pierre was the perfect suspect for us to focus on, but with everything checking out with his alibi for that night, that leaves us needing to look elsewhere," Daniel said. "So, we start all over again…at the very beginning when we first arrived at the shanty because of the frantic phone call from Angelique."

Daniel began handing out assignments of people to begin reinterviewing. Luke hated to admit it, but they had all rushed to justice in staying focused on Pierre and they had really not thought about anyone else as a viable suspect.

He hated to think about all the time he and Dominique had wasted in following Pierre and often sitting in the swamp for hours upon end while the man had hunted his prize gator or fished.

Dominique…her very name was now a sad song in his heart, an unfulfilled dream that he'd entertained for just a short moment in time.

He couldn't regret those hours wasted, for it had been those nights that had brought her into his life even if only for a brief time. He would remember the laughter in her eyes and the softness of her skin. He would forever remember their deep conversations and the fire in her kisses.

He could never regret falling in love with her, he just wished she had felt the same about him. And then what, a small voice taunted him. What was it she'd said to him? *We'd be divorced before the writing on the marriage certificate dried.*

"Luke, you with me?" Daniel's voice sliced through Luke's thoughts.

"I'm sorry, I drifted off for a moment," Luke said with a touch of embarrassment.

"Okay then, Clay, you can go ahead and take off. Luke, I'd like to see you in my office," Daniel stood.

As Clay headed out the back door, Luke followed Daniel down the long hallway. Was Daniel angry with him? Never, in all the years they'd been working together, had the two ever had words.

But his boss had evidently seen Luke daydreaming instead of focusing on the job. Once inside Daniel's office, Daniel sat at his desk and Luke sank down in the chair before him.

"I'm sorry, boss," Luke said immediately. "I've been having a little trouble focusing lately."

"Yeah, what's up with you? You've seemed a bit off your game for the last few days," Daniel replied.

Luke released a deep sigh and stared at his friend. "I made a mistake… I got too close to her. I… I'm in love with her, Daniel."

Daniel's eyes widened slightly. "And what does she have to say about all this?" he asked.

"Not much," Luke replied with a wealth of sadness. "I want to believe she's in love with me, too. But we both know it wouldn't work between us. At our very core, we are two different people who have very different needs in a partner. So now, I'm just a damn fool nursing a very broken heart."

"I'm sorry, man," Daniel replied with sympathy. "I warned you not to get too close to her, but I could see this train wreck coming from a hundred miles away."

"I got embroiled in my own thoughts a few minutes ago, but I swear I won't let that happen again," Luke replied.

Daniel reared back in his chair, his gaze thoughtful. "Maybe I should pull you off this case and put you back on regular patrol."

"Please don't do that," Luke protested as he leaned forward. "I've already put in so many hours on Mystique's murder case. I know the details and the people better than any other patrolman you might use to replace me."

"I'm assuming nothing more has happened with Dominique and the man who is after her. Otherwise, I would have heard about it," Daniel said, an obvious change of subject.

"No, nothing more has happened. My fear is that this is somehow the calm before the storm," Luke replied, his worry rife in his tone.

Daniel leaned forward, his eyes burning with a sudden anger. "Two damn cases, and we can't get a break on either one of them. I know I have smart men working for me. I know for sure we're all fine lawmen, but I'm so frustrated right now with both these cases."

"That makes two of us," Luke replied.

"Actually, I can't afford to take you off these cases, Luke. You're right, you know the details and the people far better than anyone else on the force, and you're one of my best men."

"I swear I'll be at the top of my game, Daniel. I feel like I'm personally invested in both these crimes," Luke said.

Daniel offered him a sympathetic smile. "I'm sorry about your love life, Luke. I know how much you want to find a good woman to marry. It's unfortunate that the woman you fell in love with isn't a woman who would be good for you."

Luke desperately wanted to protest Daniel's words, but ultimately, he feared his friend was right. "Thanks, man. I'll get over it." He just didn't know when he would get over her. He suspected it was going to take a very long time.

Daniel tore a piece of paper out of his notebook and handed it to Luke. "This is a list of the people I want interviewed today. Get together with Clay and decide who is doing who, and then as usual we'll meet back here at noon."

Luke stood. "Thanks, Daniel," he said and then moments later he left Daniel's office.

A call to Clay settled who each of them were interviewing and then Luke set off to interview Nola again. After that he would speak to Corrine Fortier and Helene Benoit, Jacob Benoit's older sister. All three of the women lived in the swamp and were frequent visitors of Mystique.

Luke still had his doubts that a woman would be responsible for the heinous crime, but at this point nobody could be ruled out. These women went through fairly light interviews immediately following the murder. Luke intended to press them much harder now.

By noon he'd managed to speak to all of them. Corrine and Helene both had solid alibis for the time of Mystique's murder, but the alibis would be checked to make sure they held up under tough scrutiny. Nola didn't have a solid alibi. On the night of the murder, she had been in her shanty alone.

She would be the first on the new potential suspect list, although Luke couldn't imagine the older woman murdering her best friend.

He checked in at noon and had a half an hour for a lunch break. Was Dominique working the lunch shift? It didn't matter. He wasn't going to eat there so soon after professing his love to her.

He drove through the burger place for lunch and ate in his car, his thoughts drifting back and forth between the woman he loved and the murder case.

For the next few weeks, they would be retracing footsteps they'd already taken in order to find a killer he suspected was hiding in plain sight.

He'd told the truth to Daniel when he'd said he felt as if

in Dominique's case this was the calm before the storm. He was sick at the very idea that the man who wanted to make her his own would succeed.

Stop seeing the lawman. You belong to me.

She'd stopped seeing him, although it wasn't because of the note, but the perpetrator wouldn't know that. He'd believe she had complied with his request. That thought definitely made Luke sick but there was nothing he could do about it.

All he could do was hope she remain vigilant when she was out and about. He knew she had her knife. He hoped she would use it if necessary to keep safe.

Chapter Twelve

It had been four long days since Luke had professed his love to her. Dominique felt as if she was just existing, but not enjoying life like she used to.

She went to work and then came home to the silence of her shanty…silence that had once been filled with Luke's presence. She missed him. She just hadn't expected to miss him so much.

So, she read each hour that she spent at home. She went to dinner with her sisters one night and even their chatter didn't help the wealth of loneliness that was inside of her.

She would have liked to invite Luke over and cook for him again. But knowing his feelings for her, it just wouldn't be right. A clean break was what they had needed and in the four days of working and eating out, she hadn't seen him at all.

Aside from her unsettled feelings about Luke was the ever-present fear that somebody was going to snatch her up and carry her away, and nobody would ever see or hear from her again.

She kept her knife at the ready anytime she was outside and alone. There was no way she could forget that somebody was after her. There hadn't been any more notes or anything to trouble her, but each day her fear grew more intense. Something was going to happen soon…something bad. The ominous feeling had grown inside her with each day that passed.

She now dressed for work. Tonight, she was on dinner duty. It would be a short night for her as she was only scheduled to work from four to eight.

Before she left her shanty, she grabbed her knife firmly in her hand and then set out walking. The skies overhead were as dark and dreary as her mood. The weather report was for storms moving into the area later this evening.

As she walked through the swamp, she thought about the last time it had rained. That was the night Luke had danced with her…the night he had kissed her with so much passion.

She snapped her thoughts away from the memory. *Stay focused*, she told herself. *Watch your surroundings and listen for anyone creeping close to you.*

She breathed a deep sigh of relief as she reached her car and slid in behind the wheel. She immediately pressed the button that would lock all her doors and then started up her engine.

It was only as she was driving toward the café that she allowed herself to relax a bit. And in that brief time of relaxation thoughts of Luke once again intruded into her mind.

She had a feeling she'd remember him long after she was married and had kids. She would remember the soft glow of his green eyes and the infectious nature of his grin.

She hoped to find a man who would make her laugh like Luke had, a man who would make her feel safe in his presence. Of course, he would have to be a man who could be relaxed and comfortable in her crazy schedule of no schedule.

She intended to live the lifestyle her mother had with no nod to conventional ways, and that was why Luke was definitely the wrong man for her.

Arriving at the café, she pulled into one of the few empty spaces in the lot. It looked like it was going to be a very busy dinner time. But that was good. She needed to stay busy.

Once again, she grabbed her knife as she exited the car and hurried toward the back door. She was a few minutes early for her shift, so she sank down at the table in the break room and just breathed.

It wasn't long before she was joined by a few more waitresses and then it was time to go to work. Thankfully, the dinner shift was much different than the morning and afternoon shifts since her regulars rarely showed up for dinner.

Knowing she wouldn't have to put up with the awkwardness that still marked her encounters with the three regulars caused her to relax and just enjoy doing her job.

Couples and families usually filled the café in the evenings. She always enjoyed interacting with the children who came with their parents. Their orders usually consisted of one of three things…grilled cheese, chicken nuggets or a hot dog with ice cream for dessert.

"Hi, sweetie." Nola greeted her from her seat at a four-top table. She was with two other women who smiled and nodded at her.

"How are you all doing this evening?" Dominique asked.

"We're all well, but what's wrong with you, honey?" Nola asked.

"What do you mean?" Dominique asked.

"The normal sparkle isn't in your eyes and that means something is troubling you." Nola looked at her intently. "Dominique, I've known you since you were a baby and I could always tell when something was wrong by looking at your eyes."

"Oh, it's nothing," Dominique replied with a small laugh.

"It's definitely something," Nola pressed.

"I'm just very disappointed by the murder investigation," she finally said.

"Who would have thought that Pierre was innocent," one of the other women said.

"I still don't know if I believe it or not," Nola said. "I never liked that man. He and your mom were so different and they should have never been together. All they ever did was fight with each other."

"So, what can I get for you ladies this evening?" Dominique asked, needing to get things moving so she could attend to her other tables.

They placed their orders and then Dominique left their table. That was what she and Luke would be like if they ever tried to be together, she told herself. The two of them were so different and they would probably fight all the time. It definitely wasn't a match made in Heaven.

She stayed busy for the rest of her shift and then at eight o'clock she went back into the break room to grab her purse and head home.

Once again, she pulled her knife from her purse as she stepped out of the back door of the café. The skies overhead were angry looking and there were no signs of the stars or the moon.

There was nobody around so she had nothing to worry

about. She'd had to park her car by the dumpster and she now hurried on her way to it.

She'd heard of people dumpster diving into the café's trash bin, but she'd never seen anyone actually doing that. She would like to think that in the small town of Dark Waters, nobody was hungry enough to have to seek their next meal out of the dumpster.

The only sound came from the voices that spilled out of the kitchen where the back door was open and an occasional rumble of thunder in the distance. She definitely wanted to get home before the storm was upon her.

She'd nearly reached the driver door when he appeared. Clad in dark clothes and wearing a ski mask and gloves, the man seemed to materialize out of the dark shadows.

He rushed toward her, barely giving her time to process what was happening. With her heart beating frantically, she tightened her grip on her knife.

She slashed out at him with the knife and at the same time, he lunged forward and hit her upper arm with a hypodermic needle. Whatever was in it burned as it entered her. She flailed her arm out once again as she tried to stab him, but he'd stepped back from her and was too far away for her to strike.

Danger! Danger! Get in your car and get away, a voice screamed inside her head. *Run back to the kitchen. For God's sake, do something and do it now.*

Her arms and legs felt strange, as if they were all wrapped up in cotton and wouldn't work. Her brain became too slow to process everything as she became disoriented. What was happening to her?

She knew she had to do something, but the knife slipped from her hand and clattered to the pavement. She tried to scream, but only a soft mewl escaped her.

Dizziness whirled in her head as the dark edges of unconsciousness reached out to take her. She fell into strong arms and had one last rational thought. She was in deep trouble. That was her final thought before the darkness took over and she knew no more.

Luke once again joined Daniel and Clay in the murder room as they shared and discussed what they had learned the day before with their interviews.

"I really don't believe that the women I interviewed had anything to do with the murder," Luke said. "The only connection Helene Benoit has is that Jacob Benoit is her brother, and that's connected to Dominique's case and not the murder."

"What about the men you interviewed in the afternoon?" Daniel asked.

"I spoke to all of Mystique's closest neighbors to find out if they saw or heard anything on the night of the murder. None of them did," Luke said with frustration. "Of course, Mystique's nearest neighbors aren't all that close to her shanty."

He sat back and listened as Clay gave his report. He had spoken to several of the fishermen in the swamp and he'd come up with nothing as well. Somewhere in their small town, a murderer was hiding and they were going to have to work hard to ferret him out.

There was also another man probably hiding in plain sight. He was a man besotted with Dominique and he wanted her badly. Two criminals and they couldn't find squat on either one of the cases. It was so damned frustrating.

"I hate to do this to you, but I want both of you to look at the crime scene photos again and see if you can find anything we missed." Daniel opened the file folder in front of him and began to pull out the crime scene photos.

The photos were gruesome and hard to look at, but it was part of Luke's job to thoroughly dissect them for any anomalies they might have missed. Thank God, Dominique hadn't seen any of them.

Dominique. It felt as if it had been forever since he'd seen her, although it had only been four days. It was certainly not long enough for his heartbreak to ease.

They spent the morning going over the various photos, but the pictures gave up no further information than they'd already gleaned from them.

It was just after one when they stopped working for their lunch break. Daniel went to Angelique's store where he was going to have lunch with her. Clay went home where his girlfriend had lunch ready for him.

Even though he knew it was probably a bad idea, Luke headed to the café. He didn't know if he hoped Dominique would be working or if he hoped she wasn't working the mid-shift. But it was silly to avoid the one decent place to eat in town just because he was a lovesick fool.

She was the first person he looked for when he walked through the café door. Apparently, she wasn't working this shift for he didn't see her anywhere.

He settled in at a two-top near the window and smiled at Glenda Wright as she appeared to take his order. "How are you this beautiful day, Officer Madison?"

"I'm doing just fine," he replied to the older woman. "What about you?"

"Oh, I can't complain. Now what can I get for you?"

He ordered a cheeseburger, fries and an iced tea and then stared out the window once Glenda left his table. Going over the crime scene photos that morning had reminded him of how heinous the crime against Mystique had been.

Had she been murdered by somebody who was afraid of the voodoo queen and wanted her dead? Or had it been one of the people who came to her for help?

There was no way Luke believed they had identified everyone who had visited Mystique. If they had her client book, then the investigation might have been much easier. However, without it they were just flailing in the wind.

Secrets… Mystique had dealt in secrets. She knew things about people that nobody else knew. Ultimately, was that what had gotten her killed? Had somebody been afraid that she would spill their secrets?

He continued to think about the murder as he ate his cheeseburger. Funny, it was easier to think about a crime rather than think about Dominique.

He finished eating, paid and then walked to his patrol car parked at the curb in front of the café. He was at his driver's side door when Sunny came running out of the building.

"Officer Madison," she called and ran toward him.

"Hey, Sunny." He looked at her curiously as she stopped short in front of him. "What's going on?"

"I was hoping you could tell me. Have you spoken to Dominique this morning?" she asked.

"No, I haven't. Why?" Luke's heartbeat began to race as a furrow of obvious concern fluttered across Sunny's forehead.

"She was supposed to be here today to work the mid-shift, but she didn't show up and she didn't call in, and that's not like her at all."

"Maybe she's sick? Or overslept?" Luke grasped for a logical explanation.

"To make matters even more confusing, her car is parked in the back lot."

Luke stared at her for a long moment as his stomach churned and his brain whirled with suppositions…all of them bad. "I'll check it out," he finally said.

As Sunny headed back into the café, Luke raced around the building to the parking lot. He checked out all the cars and finally spied Dominique's blue Honda parked by the dumpster.

He ran toward it, his heartbeat pounding in his head and a sense of doom crashing through him. When he reached it, he knew she'd been taken.

The air whooshed out of his lungs and he nearly fell to his knees as he saw the pink-handled knife she always carried for protection on the pavement next to the driver's side door.

He fumbled and pulled his cell phone out to call Daniel. "She's gone," he said. "Dominique has been kidnapped."

"Where are you?" Daniel asked.

"I'm next to her car in the back parking lot of the café," Luke replied as despair nearly choked him. "She's gone, Daniel. She's gone."

"Stay put. We'll be right there." Daniel hung up.

Luke hoped the whole police force showed up. They needed to find her. He didn't even know how long she'd been missing. With that thought in mind, he raced over to the café's back door. When he reached it, he asked to speak to Annie.

The older woman came to the door. "What can I do for you, Officer Madison?" She swiped a tendril of her gray hair back from her face.

"When was the last time Dominique was at work?" he asked.

"Last night. She left here a little after eight. But she didn't show up to work the mid-shift today. Is she in some kind of trouble?"

"Yes, she's in trouble," Luke replied, once again a wild despair spearing through him.

Annie frowned. "Then I hope you can get her out of trouble. She's family to us here. If I can help in any way, just let me know."

"Thanks, Annie. We may talk to you later."

Luke left the back door and returned to stand next to Dominique's car. As he stared at the knife on the pavement, tears blurred his vision.

He quickly tamped back his emotion. Crying wasn't going to get Dominique back. He needed to stay strong and focused. And where in the hell was Daniel?

Time was ticking by…precious moments they could be out there looking for her. She had to have been taken last night when she'd left the café. That meant she had already been missing for a full night and over half the day today.

He looked inside the car window but didn't see anything. He didn't want to open the vehicle or search it until Daniel showed up. He was afraid of disturbing any evidence that might be around.

Finally, he heard sirens in the distance. Within minutes, Daniel pulled in, followed by two more patrol cars. Daniel and Clay got out of Daniel's car while Officers Sam Summers, Roger Teasdale and Johnny White got out of the other cars.

Luke quickly relayed what he knew to Daniel. When he was finished, he grabbed hold of Daniel's forearm. "We have to find her, Daniel," he said desperately.

"We will, Luke. We'll find her," Daniel replied.

Luke released his hold on Daniel's arm. They had to

find her, but where did they begin to look? He watched as Daniel instructed Sam, Roger and Johnny to begin processing the car and surrounding area. Daniel then got on the phone and instructed two other officers to go to the swamp and check out Dominique's shanty.

"Clay and Luke, let's head into the station," Daniel then said.

Luke wanted to protest. He wanted to bang on doors. He wanted to tear apart every house in town and every shanty in the swamp to find her. Ultimately, he recognized they needed to go to the station and form a plan. That way they wouldn't waste more precious time.

Once again as Luke followed behind Daniel's car, his emotions roared to the forefront again. It didn't matter that she didn't love him. It didn't matter that they would never be together. All that mattered was finding her safe and sound.

Unfortunately, there was no way to know what the kidnapper was capable of. The strangled, dead bird indicated the person was capable of a brutal act. So, it was possible Dominique's very life was on the line.

Chapter Thirteen

Consciousness came slowly. The first thing she became aware of was a pounding headache. She winced and tried to climb out of the dense fog that seemed wrapped around her brain.

She attempted to open her eyes, but it was too much of an effort. What was wrong with her? She tried to gather her thoughts. She'd worked the late shift at the café. So, what had happened after that?

Suddenly, memories flooded through her brain. Walking out to her car…the masked man jumping out from behind the dumpster…the prick in her arm…and then nothing.

She gasped and sat straight up as her eyes flicked open. She released another gasp as she looked at her surroundings. She was in a bed, covered with a pink spread.

As she took in the room, her headache banged harder. It was only when she tried to raise a hand to her head that she realized her wrists were tied down.

A rope also surrounded her waist along with another rope around her ankles. She yanked on the ones holding her wrists down. Desperately, she jerked and pulled in an effort to get free, but there was no give at all in the ropes.

Who had brought her here? The door to the room was

closed and she didn't hear anything or anybody. Who had drugged her and put her in this bedroom?

She knew it was the person who had written her the notes…the man who had killed a poor bird and left it on her doorstep. Was it one of her regulars at the café, or was it somebody no one even considered?

Once again, she tugged at the ties that bound her as her veins iced with fear. Did anyone even know she'd been taken? Was anybody out looking for her? How on earth would they find her? She didn't even know where she was.

Deep sobs exploded from her as frightened tears raced down her cheeks. "Somebody help me!" She began to scream at the top of her voice. She screamed over and over again as she bucked and kicked in an effort to get free.

Finally, she collapsed back on the bed, her throat hurting and her sobs slowly halting. Surely, if anyone was nearby, they would have heard her screams.

She listened for a long moment. The room was obviously in a house, but she sensed she was all alone. She looked around again at her surroundings, hoping to see something that would give her an indication of where she was and who had taken her.

There was a small dinette table with two chairs, and a vanity with a plush bench seat. What she didn't see was anything personal and she also realized there was no window in the room.

A closet door was open and inside women's dresses hung from the hangers. Somehow the sight of the dresses terrified her almost more than anything. It was an indication that somebody had gone to a lot of trouble to make sure they could keep her here. There was another door that was closed and she assumed it might be a bathroom.

Whoever held her captive could feed her at the dinette

table. She would wear the dresses from the closet and there would never be a reason for her to leave this space.

With this thought in mind, she screamed again. She screamed as loud and as long as she could until she was finally out of breath.

Luke. Was he looking for her? Oh, how she wanted his strong arms around her now. She wanted to be enveloped by his familiar scent and feel his heart beating against her own.

If he knew she was missing, then he would be out pounding on doors and searching everywhere to find her. He would hunt for her with everything he had because he was in love with her.

She began to cry once again. She was afraid and alone and she didn't know what would happen to her. Who was going to walk through the door?

The only positive she could see in the situation was if he killed her, then she would be reunited with the mother she loved.

By the time they reached the station, Luke was beyond frantic. They went into the murder room where Daniel and Clay sat and Luke paced the floor. How could they sit when Dominique was missing? Kidnapped?

"Luke, I know this is difficult for you, but you need to keep yourself together," Daniel said.

"How are we going to find her? We have no idea where to look," Luke replied, his anguish deepening his voice. "I should have been shadowing her movements. Dammit, I should have been a real bodyguard keeping her safe."

"Right now, what we need is a game plan to find her. The first place we need to start is with the men who were her regulars at the café," Daniel said.

"Burt Stanfield, Austin Colbert and Jacob Benoit." The names tripped off Luke's tongue.

Daniel nodded. "Clay, why don't you and Roger go check out Austin Colbert. If he isn't at work at the library, go to his home." Daniel quickly looked up the address. "Call me as soon as you check him out."

"I'm off," Clay said. He stood and quickly left the room.

"Luke, you and I will see if Burt is at work today. We should be able to find him in his office. And if he isn't there, we go to his house and check it out."

This is what Luke wanted...action. "What about Jacob?"

Daniel stood and frowned. "I honestly don't think anyone who lives in the swamp has her. It would be very difficult to hold a woman there and keep it a secret."

Luke followed Daniel out of the room. Burt's office was in city hall and that building was close enough that they could walk. "I have all the men out looking for her," Daniel said as they hurried down the sidewalk.

God, they had to find her. They had no idea what the kidnapper might do to her. Hopefully, he wouldn't hurt her in any way. The thought of that happening shot a shaft of pain through Luke's heart.

They reached city hall and went inside. Daniel led him down a long hallway and then stopped and knocked on one of the closed doors.

"Enter," Burt's voice called out.

Daniel opened the door and as he and Luke walked into the office, Burt jumped up from behind his desk. "Chief LeCroix... Officer Madison," he said with surprise. "What can I do for you?"

"We have a few questions for you," Daniel replied.

"Questions about what?" Burt asked. He sank back down behind his desk and gestured them to two chairs in front of it. But Luke and Daniel remained standing.

"Dominique Santori," Daniel said.

Burt once again looked surprised. "What about her?"

"When was the last time you saw her?"

Luke stared at the man, looking for any signs of deception.

"Uh… I guess it was the day before yesterday when I went in for a late breakfast. Why? Has something happened to her?"

"She's been kidnapped," Luke blurted out.

"What?" Burt stared at Luke and then back at Daniel. "Oh my God. What can I do to help?"

"Nothing at this point," Daniel replied. "What were you doing last night around eight?"

"I was at the office working overtime to get things ready for the upcoming fall festival," Burt replied.

"Did anyone see you there?" Daniel asked.

"I'm not sure but I think Margaret Delaney might have seen me. I think she was working late that night, too," Burt said.

Luke shifted from foot to foot as a deep anxiety filled him. It was time to get moving…but get moving where?

They finally left Burt's place and headed to the café. "We need to question all the people who were working in the kitchen last night," Daniel said. "Maybe one of them saw something that might help us in our search. Whoever took her had to have had a vehicle. Maybe somebody saw it."

By that time Clay called and told them that Austin was at work in the library. His alibi was that he had been at the Voodoo Lounge the night before and it had been two days since he'd seen Dominique. Clay was headed to the bar now to check out the alibi.

When they reached the café, several of the busboys who had been at work last night were there. Daniel interviewed them one at a time, but none of them had seen or heard anything from the parking lot the night before.

It was almost seven o'clock when they went back into the station. When they walked through the front door, Angelique and Monique were there, both frantic with fear for their sister.

"Any news?" Angelique asked, her light brown eyes simmering with emotion.

"Not yet," Daniel replied.

It would be dark soon and the darkness crept into Luke's very soul. If they didn't find her soon, then this would be the second night she'd be with her kidnapper.

The very idea tortured him. What was she going through? She had to be scared out of her mind. The thought of her frightened tore him up inside.

"Luke, I've changed my mind. I think we need to head into the swamp and check out Jacob Benoit and Oliver LeBoeuf. No stone left unturned, right?"

"Right," Luke replied.

Daniel turned back to the two women. "Go home," he told them. "I promise I'll call you both with any news we get. There's nothing you can do here."

He reached out and touched Angelique's cheek. It was the same way Luke had touched Dominique and it brought the sting of tears to his eyes.

The four of them left the station together. Angelique and Monique headed to their homes and Luke and Daniel with three other patrolmen headed for the swamp.

Luke was grateful Daniel turned on his lights and

siren, indicating it was an emergency. It *was* an emergency. It didn't take long for them to reach the swamp entrance.

They all got out of their cars and pulled flashlights against the encroaching twilight shadows. Daniel led the way and the rest of the men followed him on the narrow path.

They had been to both men's shanties before. Both were small. All they'd have to do was open the front doors and it would instantly be known if Dominique was being held in one of them.

Let her be here, Luke prayed. *Let her be here so we can rescue her and take her home.* They would arrest the kidnapper and she'd never have to worry again. And let her be okay.

At the idea of the kidnapper harming her in any way, a rage momentarily stole the fear from Luke. Who was this creep who thought it was okay to take a woman from her life and those who loved her?

It didn't take long to learn that Dominique wasn't in either of the shanties. Neither man had a solid alibi for the night before, but it didn't matter. She wasn't there.

As they headed back to their cars, a new, deep despair took hold of Luke. They had checked all the men who had been on their suspect list and had come up with nothing.

Where did they go from here? How on earth were they going to find her? A dreadful thought shot through his head. What if they never found her?

IT FELT AS if she'd been alone and tied to the bed forever. Without a window in the room, it was impossible for her to see what time it might be. She didn't even know if it was day or night.

She continued to pull and tug at the restraints until her wrists were raw and burned from her efforts and she became breathless and had to rest.

She didn't scream anymore. She'd realized there was no point in it. She'd screamed enough already and nobody had come to help her. Wherever she was, there apparently wasn't anyone else around.

What she did know was she wasn't in the swamp anymore. This room smelled faintly of sawdust and paint, not the sweet green and floral scents of her home.

When she was exhausted by her exertions, her thoughts ran free. She thought about her life. She thought about her mother's murder and the loss and grief she still felt. Finally, she thought about Luke.

She was in the midst of thoughts about him when she heard the sound of a door slamming shut. Heavy footsteps came closer and she tensed with terror. Who was going to come through the door? Who had done this to her and what did they want with her?

The steps came closer and closer and then a lock clicked and the door slowly crept open. He stepped into the room. "You," she gasped in stunned surprise.

He smiled at her. "Hi, Dominique. You really belong to me now." He pulled out one of the chairs at the table and sank down.

"Please, you need to let me go. This isn't the way to go about things," Dominique said feverishly. "Untie me and let me go and you won't be in any trouble."

"I'll untie you when you're truly ready to be my wife," he replied. He leaned forward. "Oh, Dominique, I've been so lonely. You know I'm crazy about you. Now, are you hungry? I have a nice steak for dinner for us this evening."

She stared at his familiar face. Had he lost his mind?

She was tied up in a bed after having been kidnapped and he was talking about steak for dinner?

"Actually, what I'd like is to use the restroom," she replied. He would have to untie her and maybe she would be able to get away.

"Of course." He jumped up out of the chair and moved to her side. She remained frozen in place as he untied first her wrists, then the rope around her waist and finally the one that had kept her legs from moving.

"You shouldn't have to be tied up after today," he said as she sat up and swung her legs over the side of the bed.

"That would be nice," she replied evenly. Maybe untied she could figure out a way out of this nightmare. He gestured toward the closed door. "The bathroom is right there."

She stood a bit unsteadily. She stayed in place until the pins and needles in her feet and legs stopped. After being in the same position all day, they all had gone numb.

"Feel free to use the shower in there whenever you want, and there is a large variety of dresses in the closet for you to wear." He beamed a smile at her. "I'm particularly partial to the yellow dress."

He stood. "Oh, Dominique, we're going to have a wonderful life together. Now, I'll be back with our dinner very soon." With that he walked to the door, stepped out and when he closed it behind him she heard a lock fall into place.

Slowly, she walked into the small bathroom. She needed to find a weapon…something she could use to disable him so she could escape.

In the bathroom there was a stool, a sink and a shower with a bar of soap on the floor. There was no mirror that could be broken and no window to crawl through.

She left the bathroom and began to explore the rest of the bedroom. The vanity held nothing but a plastic bristle brush. There was absolutely nothing in the room that could be used as a weapon.

She sank down on the bed. *Oh, Dominique, we're going to have a wonderful life together.* His words played and replayed in her head. The man was obviously delusional.

Maybe she could rush him at the door when he came back in. He would probably be carrying a couple of plates of food. It might be her only chance to escape.

With this thought in mind, she moved to position herself just inside the door. He was bigger than her, but she would have the element of surprise on her side.

She gathered every inch of strength she had inside her. She would fight like a wildcat to get away. This had to work…it just had to!

She remained in position as minutes ticked by. She didn't know how long she waited before she heard his footsteps coming back. She tensed, adrenaline rushing through her veins.

She heard the click of the door being unlocked and when he came through, she screamed and pushed to get past him. The plates he was carrying fell to the floor as he grabbed her by the shoulders and shoved her back into the room.

She punched and kicked, still trying desperately to get through the door. He reared his arm back and hit her on her chin, the blow careening her backward as a horrendous pain stabbed through her jaw. She stumbled and fell to the floor on her hands and knees, panting from the exertion of her unsuccessful efforts.

"I don't tolerate disobedience," he said angrily. "Now, your dinner is all over the floor and that's where you can eat it." He stepped out of the doorway, slammed the door and then locked it once again.

Dominique slowly pulled herself up off the floor, silently weeping with pain and frustration. She sank down on the side of the bed as an icy chill walked up her spine. She now knew the man was not only delusional, but dangerous as well.

Chapter Fourteen

The nighttime hours passed in agonizing increments as Luke remained at the police station. He and Daniel had interviewed everyone who might be guilty and they'd come up empty-handed.

It was just after two in the morning, and Luke paced back and forth in the break room, his heart absolutely bleeding with the need to find her. Daniel was in his office, working to figure out where they went next. He had all the night force driving the streets and keeping an eye out for the missing woman.

However, Luke knew they had no place to go next. Luke now believed somebody who had not been on their suspect list was responsible. Hell, that could be almost any male in town.

It had been around ten when Adam Kincaid, one of the night cops, had driven through to get burgers for everyone. Luke's burger remained untouched on the table. How could he eat when Dominique was missing? He had no appetite, except for his intense hunger to find Dominique.

Daniel had tried to get him to go home and get some sleep, but Luke refused to leave. He needed to be here in case something happened.

The last thing he wanted was for any of the night crew

to find her on the street because that would mean they had found her body. Once again, he prayed that the person who had taken her didn't hurt her.

He threw himself into a chair at the table and stared unseeing at the wall. Instead, he saw Dominique's beautiful face and her gorgeous smile. Visions of her laughing and dancing in the rain, of her eyes sparkling so bright, rushed through his head.

He must have nodded off for he jerked awake as some of the day cops entered the break room. Morning. And still she was gone.

For the next two days they interviewed more people who had been in the café on the night she was taken. They spoke to more of the swamp people, but nobody had any news for them. It was as if a UFO had beamed her up without a trace.

During those two days, Luke ate only what he needed to keep going. He dozed in the murder room, what little sleep he got troubled and full of nightmares. He went to his home twice, just long enough to shower and change clothes.

Finally, desperate for answers, at nine in the morning he drove to the swamp wanting to touch base with Jacque LeBlanc. Jacque himself was shrouded in mystery. Nobody knew where he'd come from or anything personal about him. Luke didn't care about any of that. What he did care about was the man was rumored to know what was going on in the swamp.

Jacque's shanty was secluded but Luke had been there before when he and Daniel had first spoken to the man about Mystique's murder.

This time, Luke was by himself as he made his way through the swamp. It was difficult for him to focus on anything but Dominique. He just wanted her to be found. He couldn't imagine going on for the rest of his life not knowing what had happened to her.

Jacque's shanty came into view and Luke hurried his footsteps to the front door. "Jacque, it's Officer Madison," he shouted as he knocked on the door.

The dark-haired, well-built man opened the door. "Officer Madison. How can I help you?"

"I'd like to ask you a few questions. Can I come in?"

The gator-hunter opened his door wider to allow Luke entry. The shanty was spotlessly clean with a dark gray sofa and chair and a large bookcase filled with books on all types of subjects. Definitely unusual in the world of gator-hunters.

"Please, have a seat." Jacque gestured to the sofa. Luke nodded and sat. "Now, questions about what?"

"I don't know if you've heard or not, but Dominique Santori was kidnapped three nights ago," Luke said.

"Oh, I've heard. The swamp has been buzzing with the news. Dominique and her sisters are well-liked here," Jacque replied.

Luke leaned forward. "Have you heard anything that might help us find her?"

"I'm afraid not. But I can tell you that I don't believe she is being held here in the swamp. All the fishermen and gator-hunters are genuinely worried about her and secrets are hard to keep here," Jacque said.

"I'm worried sick about her," Luke replied, his desperation ringing in his voice.

Jacque gazed at him sharply. "It's like that?"

Luke offered the man a weak smile. "It's like that," he replied.

"I really wish I could help you, but I haven't heard anything."

"I knew it was a long shot," Luke replied and stood. "Thanks for your time."

"No problem." Jacque walked with him to the door. "I hope you find her safe and sound." For a moment Jacque's green eyes darkened. "Because there's nothing worse than losing somebody you love."

"Thanks again." Luke walked slowly away from the shanty, despair once again filling his heart…his very soul. It had been so long now, too long. Three nights she'd been with her kidnapper unless he'd already… He snapped his thoughts away from that torturous thought. It couldn't be too late to save her. It just couldn't be.

It was just about ten o'clock when he arrived back at the station. In the murder room, half a dozen officers were gathered along with Daniel and Clay.

"Luke," Daniel greeted him. "We've decided to start a grid search of the town. I want officers knocking on doors and asking questions," he said. "What I need you to do is go to the café. Annie called a few minutes ago and said she'd put together a platter of sweet rolls and pastries for the officers. We'll put it in the break room where they can grab one and go. So, if you want to head over there now, I'd appreciate it."

"I'll go right now."

He left the murder room and headed back to his patrol car. It took him only minutes to arrive and park in the café's lot where Dominique's car was still parked by the dumpster. The sight of it wrenched his heart.

This was the crime scene, but it had yielded no answers. They had used a locksmith to get into the car, but nothing of value had been found inside. The entire area had been meticulously searched and the officers had found nothing useful.

He was slowly losing hope and that frightened him. He headed around the building to the front door. He stopped just inside the entrance and gazed around, somehow seeking her where he knew she wouldn't be. He didn't know how long he'd been standing there when Sunny approached him.

"Officer Madison, can I help you?" she asked softly.

"Yeah, I was sent to pick up a platter that Annie prepared for the men at the station," he replied.

"Oh yes, it's in the break room. She has it all ready to go. Just follow me."

He walked behind Sunny and she led him to the small break room. Lockers lined one wall. There was a round table and in the center of it was a large platter of breakfast sweets wrapped in plastic.

"No news yet?" Sunny asked.

"None," Luke replied grimly.

Sunny lightly touched Luke's shoulder. "I know you miss her…we all do. All her regulars ask about her every day—well, all of them but Burt."

"He doesn't ask about her?" Luke asked in surprise.

"He hasn't been in for breakfast since she disappeared." She leaned over the table and grabbed the large platter. "Here you are," she said as she handed it to him. "I hope all the officers enjoy it."

"Thanks, and please tell Annie thank you. It was very thoughtful of her to do this," he replied.

"I'll tell her." She walked with him back to the front door. "You have to find her, Luke." Sunny's blue eyes filled with tears.

"We're doing everything possible," he replied, emotion rising up inside him. "I'll see you later." He hurried out the front door before he embarrassed himself by blubbering in front of Sunny.

Dominique was missing and he was picking up pastries from the café. He had a feeling Daniel was just trying to keep him busy, but he didn't want to be the errand guy, he needed to be involved in the search.

As he pulled out of the café parking lot to head back to the station, something niggled in the back of his brain, but he didn't know what it was.

He arrived back and carried the platter inside to the break room, where he placed it in the center of the table. Nobody was in there at the moment and there was nobody in the murder room. Apparently, all the officers had left to begin the grid search.

He found Daniel in his office and sank down in the chair across from him. "The platter is here. Now you need to tell me where to go to help in the search."

"Luke, you're exhausted. You haven't really slept or eaten in days. You need to go home and get some rest and leave the search to the other men."

"You know I can't do that," Luke replied. "I need to be here in case something breaks." He frowned, the niggling feeling back inside his head. Somehow, he was missing something…something that could be important. The thought suddenly unfolded in his brain.

"Burt," he said, his heart beat beginning to race.

"What about him?" Daniel looked at him curiously.

"I spoke briefly to Sunny when I was at the café. She told me Burt hadn't been in since Dominique went missing. Why isn't he going in to eat his breakfast as usual?"

"He had an alibi for the night in question," Daniel protested.

"An alibi we didn't check," Luke said. He realized in the thick of things, they hadn't followed up on Burt's alibi. "We checked his alibi but we didn't follow up on it and we didn't check out his house." Luke leaned forward, a new burst of adrenaline rushing through him. "Daniel, we need to get inside his house."

"We'll head to his office and get him to come with us and let us in to look around. I'll contact Judge Blakely and see if he'll sign off on a search warrant for Burt's place."

"We need to go there as soon as possible," Luke replied, his stomach churning. "Can't we just go there and break down the door?"

"Luke, the last thing we want to do is jeopardize the case. We do things by the book. Give me five minutes to cross my t's and dot my i's so we don't make any mistakes. Wait for me in the lobby and when I'm done here, we'll go talk to Burt."

Luke walked out to the lobby, where Gus sat behind the desk. "How are you doing, Luke?" the older man asked.

"I'm okay," Luke replied. But of course, he wasn't okay. He began to pace, his thoughts on the possibility that Burt might be their kidnapper.

Was this just another wild-goose chase? Was he taking a casual statement from a waitress and making too big a deal out of it? He didn't know. All he did know for sure was that they needed to check this out.

Daniel joined him and together the two men swiftly walked to city hall. "I got hold of Judge Blakely but he wouldn't sign off on a search warrant. We don't have enough evidence for one. We'll just have to hope Burt lets us in without needing the warrant."

"All I know is I want to get into his house as quickly

as possible," Luke replied. "If she's not there, then at least it's one place we cleared."

They reached city hall and headed down the hallway to Burt's office. When they reached it, Daniel knocked firmly on the door. There was no response. Daniel knocked again, this time louder. "Burt, it's Chief LeCroix," he called.

The door to the office next to Burt's opened up. "He's not there," Margaret Delaney, the city clerk, said.

"Do you know where he's at?" Luke asked.

"I'm assuming he's at home. He called in sick this morning," she replied.

The tension in Luke's body tightened. Was he right about this? It felt right. *Please let it be right.* He turned and practically ran out of the building with Daniel hot on his heels.

When they reached the police station they got into Daniel's car to head to Burt's place. As they drove, Daniel called in several more officers to meet them there.

Luke's heart beat so hard it felt as if it might explode out of his chest. Hope surged up inside him, a hope he prayed wouldn't be dashed by the end of this search.

By the time they reached Burt's house, a rich adrenaline flooded Luke's veins. Burt's house was a ranch located at the back of a dead end. On one side some distance away was a house that was obviously abandoned and on the other side was another ranch house, also some distance away. There was a red pickup truck in the driveway, indicating that Burt was home.

Before he could get out of the car, Daniel grabbed his arm to hold him in place. "We go in slow, Luke. If she's in there, the last thing we want is for any sort of a hostage situation to unfold."

Luke nodded. Even though he was ready to storm the door, he knew Daniel was right. They didn't know if Burt would be armed and they didn't know where, exactly, in the house Dominique might be located. The best they could do was get Burt out of the house before they went in to search.

The last thing he wanted was to do anything that might put Dominique at more risk if she was inside the house. They sat and waited until two more patrol cars pulled up. Together, they all got out of their cars.

Daniel instructed two of the officers to wait near the front door and he told Clay to head around the back of the house and guard the door there.

With everything in place, Daniel and Luke approached the front door. Daniel knocked and Luke held his breath. *Please let her be inside,* he inwardly prayed.

Daniel knocked again. "Burt, it's Chief LeCroix."

After several moments, the lock on the front door sounded and then Burt opened the door. "Chief… Officer Madison, what's going on?" He appeared confused as he gazed at them.

"We have a few more questions to ask you," Daniel said. "Can we come in?"

"Uh…it's really not a good time right now." He offered them an easy smile. "I've been doing a little cleaning and, in the process, I've made quite a mess in my living room. But I'll be glad to answer any questions you might have." He stepped out on the porch and closed the door behind him. "Now, what can I help you with?"

"Burt, we'd really like to come in and search your place," Daniel said. "We're checking all the homes of people Dominique was close to."

"Well you aren't checking mine without a search warrant," Burt replied.

"Chief, I think I heard somebody cry for help inside," Johnny said. "I think we need to go in."

"That's a damn lie," Burt exclaimed. "You can't hear anything."

"I'm telling you, I hear a woman crying for help," Johnny said.

"I heard it, too," Roger said.

Daniel motioned the two officers, Roger and Johnny, forward. "Burt, you need to turn around. Roger is going to cuff you. You aren't under arrest, but you are detained while we do a complete search of your house."

"A search of my house?" Burt jerked against Roger, who successfully got him in handcuffs. "What on earth is wrong with you people? What right do you have to do this to me? You need a damned search warrant."

"Not if we think somebody is in imminent danger," Daniel replied.

Luke shoved Burt out of the way, opened the door and walked in. Rather than things being a mess, the living room was neat and tidy. He heard nothing to indicate that there was a woman being held prisoner inside, but that didn't mean she wasn't here. He was grateful that Johnny and Roger had given them a reason come on inside.

Daniel entered the house as well, but Luke was three steps ahead of him as he ran down the hallway. The house appeared to have three bedrooms and all the doors to those rooms were closed.

Luke ripped open the door to the first one. Masculine furniture and a brown plaid spread on the king-size bed let him know this was probably Burt's bedroom.

As he stepped out of the bedroom, he saw it. On the door on the left end of the hallway was a lock. It was a simple hasp lock. Why would somebody put that on the outside of a bedroom door—unless they wanted to keep somebody inside?

He gasped and raced to the door. He disengaged the hasp lock and then opened it. His heart nearly wept with relief. Thank God, she was there. She was tied to the bed. "Luke!" she cried out at the sight of him.

He rushed to her side, along with Daniel. "It's okay, Dominique. We're here now and you're safe," Luke said as he began to work the ropes to untie her. She was clad in an ill-fitting red dress and her hair was a tangle around her head. She began to cry and tears of relief burned at his eyes.

Together, he and Daniel finally got her untied. She jumped out of the bed and fell into Luke's arms. He closed his eyes and held her tight, breathing in the very scent of her as he reveled in the fact that she was alive.

She continued to weep until Daniel interrupted. "I've got an ambulance on the way," he said.

"I… I just want to go home," she said.

Luke looked her over. When he saw the bruise on her jaw, a rage nearly overwhelmed him. She'd been hit. And she'd been hit hard.

"Dominique, you need to go to the hospital and get checked out," he said softly.

She gazed at him and then nodded. At that moment, a siren screamed in the air. "That will be the ambulance," Daniel said.

Together, the three of them walked outside with Dominique clinging to Luke's arm. "Dominique, I did this because I love you," Burt yelled out.

Without warning, Luke stepped up to the man and hit him hard in his jaw. Burt's head snapped back with the blow and he gasped with obvious pain.

"Did you all see that? It was police brutality. I'll sue you all for that," he yelled.

"What I saw was a kidnapper trying to escape," Johnny replied easily.

"Yeah, that's what I saw, too," Roger added.

"Liars!" Burt exclaimed, his face reddened with anger. "You're all a bunch of liars."

"Good luck proving that in a court of law," Johnny said.

"Don't try to escape again. I'll just have to subdue you with another punch to your face," Luke warned, his anger as he stared at the man nearly out of control.

"Take him to jail," Daniel said.

"With pleasure," Roger said.

"And then come back here to help process the scene," Daniel added.

Luke led Dominique to the awaiting ambulance, where the two EMT's attended to her. Once she was loaded up, the ambulance pulled away. Luke stared after the vehicle.

Intense relief nearly cast him to the ground. Hopefully, she had no other physical injuries than the bruised jaw, which was bad enough. But it would heal and eventually she would be fine.

"Go," Daniel said from behind him. Luke turned to look at his friend. "I know you want to go with her. We can handle things here." He tossed his car keys to Luke. "I can catch a ride back to the station later. And in the meantime, I'll give her sisters a call. I'm sure they'll meet you there."

"Thanks," Luke replied and then raced for Daniel's

car. Once in it, he turned on the siren and then hurried to catch up with the ambulance.

They arrived at the hospital at the same time. Dominique was taken to the emergency room bay and Luke parked and then ran for the hospital's front door.

Once inside, he checked in with the receptionist and told her he wanted to speak with Dominique's doctor when he finished checking her out.

He then sank down in one of the plastic chairs in the waiting room. For the first time in what felt like forever, he was able to breathe.

He leaned his head back against the wall as a deep wave of exhaustion struck him. She was safe. Finally, she'd been found. It was as if he'd been missing a large chunk of his heart but now that chunk had been restored.

Love for her flooded through his veins, warming the icy chill that had been inside him since the moment they had discovered her gone.

He wasn't alone in the waiting room for long. Angelique and Monique joined him there. "Thank God, you found her," Angelique said, her eyes misty with tears as she hugged Luke.

"We've been so afraid," Monique added, tears of relief also shimmering in her eyes.

They sank down in the chairs next to him. "Have you heard anything yet?" Angelique asked.

"No, nothing," he replied.

"Daniel told me she has a large bruise on her jaw. He also told me you gave Burt a bruised jaw," Angelique said.

"I hope I broke his damned jaw," he confessed.

"So do we," Monique said with a small smile. She sobered. "I can't believe it was Burt, a well-respected man who works for the city."

"I'm just glad she's safe now." Once again, love for her filled his heart.

The three of them sat in the waiting room for about an hour and finally Dr. Gregory Harmon stepped in. They all stood at the sight of the older doctor.

"How is she?" Angelique asked before Luke could.

"She has a bruised jaw, but thankfully nothing was broken. She is dehydrated and exhausted. I'm keeping her overnight so she can rest and we can get some fluids in her."

"Can we see her?" Luke asked.

"I've given her a mild sedative and she's already sleeping. I would prefer she not be awakened. I imagine she'll just be here for one night. As long as there are no complications, she'll be released tomorrow. You can all see her then."

A swift disappointment swept through Luke. He'd just wanted to see her…maybe hold her hand and assure himself that she was truly okay. But, if she was resting peacefully, he also didn't want to disturb her.

The three of them walked out of the hospital together. They said their goodbyes and then Luke got into his car. He dropped his forehead on the steering wheel and the tears he'd fought back for the past three days began to fall.

Each tear washed away the terror he'd had since the moment she'd been kidnapped. The tears were thanks to the vast relief that she'd been found alive.

He finally pulled himself together and called Daniel. He updated Daniel on Monique's condition and told him that both her sisters had come to the hospital and had gone home. "I'm just now leaving the hospital and can be back at Burt's house in about fifteen minutes."

"You are not to come here," Daniel said firmly. "I

don't need you here. I have plenty of officers to process the scene. I want you to go home, Luke. Get something to eat and get some sleep."

"I have to admit, that sounds like a great idea. Then, I'll be in as usual in the morning," he replied.

The two men hung up and Luke pulled out of the hospital parking lot. Night had fallen as it was almost nine o'clock. Tonight, the darkness of night was soothing, unlike the last three when the darkness had been torturous knowing that Dominique was out there somewhere all alone with a kidnapper.

He drove through and got himself a burger and fries and then headed home. Suddenly, he was ravenous and the added bonus was that he knew tonight he would sleep peacefully, knowing Dominique was safe and sound.

Chapter Fifteen

Dominique awakened to the scents of bacon and eggs and fresh coffee. She raised the head of the hospital bed, hoping that meant she was going to get some breakfast soon. She was definitely hungry. She really hadn't eaten anything while she'd been held.

Burt Stanfield. She still found it hard to believe that the man who had joked with her, the man who had appeared to be hardworking and kind, had kidnapped her.

It was only a few minutes later that Daniel and Luke walked into her room. Luke looked so achingly handsome in his uniform and her heart squeezed tight in her chest at the sight of him.

"Dominique, how are you feeling?" Daniel asked.

"Amazingly well…except for the pain in my jaw," she replied and then smiled at Luke. "And thank you for giving Burt a pain in his jaw."

"I would have liked to give him more," Luke replied with the boyish grin that always made her heart beat a little faster.

"If you're up to it, we need to get an official statement from you detailing everything that happened from the moment you were taken."

"I'm up to it," she replied.

Daniel pulled a mini recorder from his pocket and she started talking. She began from the moment Burt had attacked her in the café parking lot.

"He talked about his dead wife and how the silence in his house since then was driving him crazy," she said. "I was a replacement for her. He believed she'd broken her promise to be with him forever by dying. He had all her clothes for me to wear."

She told them about trying to escape and Burt hitting her. "I knew then that he could get violent so I tried to be as quiet and compliant as possible when he was in the bedroom. But when he wasn't in the room, I continued to look for a way to escape or some sort of weapon I could use against him. Unfortunately, I was unsuccessful on both counts."

She offered a bright smile to both men. "But all's well that ends well, right?"

"Right," Daniel replied. "But I have one last, very personal question for you."

She tensed. "Okay, what is it?"

"Did Burt hurt you in any other way, assault you physically, sexually?" he asked.

"No, thank God he didn't," she replied. "But I'm sure that was in his plans. Only in his head it wouldn't be an assault. He'd believe it would be a mutual decision no matter how much I kicked and screamed. He was definitely delusional in his thinking."

"Thanks, Dominique. I think I got enough from you. Burt is going to go away for a very long time," Daniel assured her.

"That's good news for me," she replied. She kept her gaze focused on Daniel. For some reason, looking at Luke hurt.

At that time an older woman Dominique didn't know

pushed in a cart with her breakfast. "Bacon and eggs, toast and orange juice for our patient," she said as she placed the plate on a table she pulled out over Dominique's lap.

"I hope there's also some coffee," Dominique said.

The woman grinned at her. "Definitely I have coffee for you."

"We'll just go now and let you eat your breakfast in peace," Daniel said. "I know you'll be available if I have further questions."

"Of course," she replied and then she looked at Luke. His gaze was soft and full of love. And then the two men left.

As she ate, a sadness filled her. It was the same sadness that had been with her since the moment Luke had spoken of his love for her.

She had spent a lot of time while she'd been held captive thinking about him and thinking about her mother. By the time she finished eating, Dr. Harmon came in.

"How's my patient today?" he asked with a kindly smile.

"I'm good and ready to get home," she replied.

"I don't see a reason to keep you any longer, so I'll have my nurse prepare your discharge paperwork and then you're free to go."

"Thank you, Dr. Harmon," she replied.

When he left the room, she used the hospital telephone on the nightstand to call Monique. Her sister not only agreed to come and get her, but also agreed to bring her some clothes. When Dominique had been rescued, she'd been wearing one of the dresses from the closet.

An hour later, she walked out of the hospital with both

her sisters at her side. They fawned over her until she assured them both she was just fine.

Within minutes, they were at the swamp's entrance. "Do you want us to walk you in?" Angelique asked as Monique parked.

"No, I'll be fine, and I know you both need to get back to work," she replied.

"We're just so grateful to have you back with us," Angelique said.

The three of them hugged and said their goodbyes and then Dominique began the trek home.

It was wonderful to be able to walk through the swamp without a knife clutched in her hand and without fear in her heart. This, more than anything, made her realize her ordeal was truly over.

By all accounts, Pierre was innocent in her mother's murder and the person who had been after Dominique was under arrest. She no longer needed Luke as her bodyguard. She probably wouldn't see him much anymore. Once again, a wave of sadness filled her heart.

She reached her shanty. Since she didn't have her purse, she had no key, but thankfully she had one hidden under a rock at the foot of her bridge. She retrieved it and then used it to go inside where she sank down in the corner of the sofa.

She didn't have her cell phone. Eventually, she'd have to buy a new one. She'd also need to get a driver's license and other things that had been in her wallet. She needed to check in at the café and get back on the schedule to work. And she'd have to make arrangements for one of her sisters to take her to get her car which was in the police station parking lot. It had been towed there for further processing following her disappearance. But not today.

Today, she just wanted to rest and revel in the fact that she was free and didn't need to be afraid anymore. There would be no more troubling notes or anything else left at her shanty door. And no more Luke.

Unable to sit still for long, she passed the afternoon by cleaning. She wiped down the cabinets in the kitchen area and then mopped the floors. After that, she changed the sheets on her bed.

By that time, she was hungry and so she started the generator and hunted in the cooler for something she could cook. The ice inside was nearly gone. She'd have to throw most of the food away and go shopping.

She made herself a grilled cheese and ate it with some chips and a soda. She had just finished eating when there was a knock on her door.

It was Luke. At the sight of him, her heart expanded. "Luke," she greeted him in surprise.

"Hi, Dominique," he replied.

"Come in." She opened the door enough so he could walk in. It was only then that she saw her purse in his hand.

"We found this at Burt's place. It looks like everything is still inside it. Your phone and driver's license are inside and I knew you'd need them back as soon as possible." He held the purse out to her.

"Thank you," she replied. "Can you sit for a few minutes?" she asked.

"Okay." He walked over to the sofa as she dug into the purse to retrieve her phone.

"Let me just plug this in to charge and I'll be right back." She hurried into the kitchen to take care of the phone, then returned to the living room and sank down next to him. Instantly, she was surrounded by his familiar scent…the one that had always made her feel safe and protected.

"How are you doing?" he asked. His eyes filled with a wealth of concern. "Does your jaw hurt badly?"

"Not too badly," she replied. She looked away from him and instead gazed across the room. "Luke, I did a lot of thinking in the three days I was gone. I thought a lot about my mother and I realized something really important." She gazed back at him. "In my grief, I've been trying to live the wild and free life she always had. I guess I felt that if I was just like her, then she wouldn't really be dead."

"Oh, Dominique," he said softly.

She heard it. When he said her name, she heard the love. When she gazed in his eyes, she saw his love. And in her time alone, she had realized the depths of her love for him. Her love for him was what had caused the sadness inside her, but she wasn't sad anymore.

She held his gaze for a long moment. "If I'm not working the late shift at the café, I could have your dinner on the table at six every night," she blurted.

He looked at her in surprise and then that wonderful smile curved his lips. "I don't have to eat at six o'clock every night. I could eat earlier or later, depending on your schedule. I could definitely cook for you, too."

Hope lit up the gold flecks in his beautiful green eyes. Hope filled her heart, her very soul.

"Luke, we've been a couple of fools," she said. "I know we can make it work between us. If we both give a little, I think we could be very happy together forever."

He grabbed her hand, stood and pulled her up and into his arms. "Are you trying to tell me you love me?" he asked, his hope shimmering in his eyes.

"Oh Luke, I am wildly, madly in love with you." She barely got the words out before his mouth took hers in a long, slow kiss that spoke of a happy future together.

When the kiss ended, she remained in his arms, reluctant to move away. He gazed deeply into her eyes. "There was a time I didn't think I could live with you, but now I know I can't live without you," he said.

Her heart swelled with her love for this man who had been her bodyguard, her friend and her lover. "I will do what I can to adhere to your schedules," she said.

"And I will dance in the rain with you and be ready for your spontaneity any time of the day or night," he replied. His gaze grew more serious. "I also intend to work hard to solve your mother's murder. I promise you, Dominique. I won't stop until we get justice for her."

She placed a hand on his lower jaw. "I know that. Somehow, I wonder if it was her magic that brought us together. I mean, without me believing Pierre was guilty and running with my scheme to bring him down, you and I probably wouldn't have ever spent any time together."

"Thank God for Mystique's magic," he replied, his gaze once again soft and loving on her.

She ran a finger over his lower lip. "Want to see what kind of magic we could make in my bedroom?" she asked, wanting nothing more than to truly make love with the man of her heart.

"There's that spontaneity in you again," he said teasingly. "I'll definitely roll with this one." He took her hand and pulled her toward her bedroom.

There would be things they'd need to figure out later, like where they were going to live and other logistics, but for now, that was the last thing on her mind, as she knew they'd conquer anything as long as they were together.

Epilogue

Monique sat on her small deck and watched the sunrise awaken the swamp. She sipped her cup of coffee as brilliant rays of gold and pink and orange lit up the eastern sky.

The colors reflected on the water as morning birds began to sing from the trees. Nocturnal creatures would be going to bed while others would be waking up for another day.

She should be at complete peace in this moment of solitude. Dominique had been rescued safe and sound and that's what she had prayed for.

However, she wasn't at peace. It had been three months now since her mother had been viciously murdered and there was no suspect in sight.

She loved her work at All That Jazz and she loved her life in her quiet, peaceful shanty. But she desperately needed closure in her mother's murder. She needed justice to be done in order to make her feel whole.

Right now, there were ragged holes in her heart and she knew they wouldn't heal until her mother's murderer was arrested and put behind bars.

Angelique had tried to solve the crime by questioning potential suspects. Dominique, certain that Pierre was guilty, had put herself at risk by shadowing the gator-hunter.

Maybe it was time Monique formulated a plan to find the person who had killed her mother by slashing her throat. Obviously, the police had no clues to follow.

She took the last drink of her coffee. The sun was up and a plan had begun to brew in her head. It would be dangerous, but something had to be done and maybe it was up to her to help the police.

All she knew for sure was the anxiety that fluttered through her most of the time and the missing piece of her heart was due to the fact that nobody had been arrested for the crime.

The only way to fix both those things was for her to do what she could to finally solve the case once and for all. She got up from her chair, set her cup to the side and started up her generator.

Nervous energy filled her, along with a simmering sense of anticipation. It was time for her to begin her day, but tonight when she got off of work, she would set her plan into motion.

* * * * *